STARERS

Nathan Robinson

The Old Man At The Bus Stop In The Rain

All it took to persuade Dylan Keene to head to his local pub; *The Green Tree,* after a hard week's graft was a simple argument. This is what he had done with his unappreciative family; now as he nursed his fourth Guinness with a Jameson chaser dropped in for good measure, the anger and frustration he felt towards his should-be loved ones had been dampened, temporarily of course. His best mate Harry had sent a four lettered text message that the majority of most hardworking men loved, sealing the deal.

PINT?

After a near six-hundred mile round trip to Pontypool, Dylan was more than ready for a pint or two or three.

'So let me get this straight,' his younger brother Lennon queried, 'she was at school right?'

'Yeah, in a cupboard with some lad.' Dylan took a thoughtful sip of the black meal in a glass, licked his lips and placed the drink carefully back down on the soggy beer mat.

'They were naked?' Harry Price, Lennon's and Dylan's joint best friend since junior school added with a quizzical eyebrow.

'No not naked,' Dylan reiterated, 'how did the deputy head put it? *"They were found with their hands in each other's pants, except they weren't wearing pants,"* something along those lines.'

Harry and Lennon sucked air in through their teeth and grimaced.

'You must've exploded on her?' Harry asked.

'Yeah, I called her a . . .' Dylan paused, catching the word before it left his lips. 'It doesn't matter what I called her. It wasn't nice.'

'She still got that four-haircuts at once thing going on?' Harry rolled his hands around his head as if he was wearing an imaginary fishbowl upon his shoulders, then spiked up his fingers.

'Yeah, she's now talking about a sculptured Mohawk next, after she watched The Girl with a Dragon Tattoo over at her friend's house,' Dylan revealed with a roll of the eyes.

'You remember when Dyl went through his Goth stage? The long hair and makeup?' Lennon asked Harry, giving him a nudge.

Harry nodded and smiled. 'Didn't that paedo think you were a little girl or something?'

'I was mistaken for a girl and offered a lift by a stranger, yes that is true.' Dylan admitted without too much reluctance. 'And yes, I shaved my head the day after so the mistake wasn't ever repeated.' Dylan ran a hand over his shorn scalp, then said with a smile, 'and I've kept it that way ever since, saves me time in the morning and old men don't try and fuck me.'

'Didn't he try it again after you shaved your head because he still fancied you?'

'No, Len, he didn't. But you like to remember it that way. Besides, I'm not a Goth no more; I'm a smiley person.'

'How old is Lucy now?' Harry asked with a scratch of his beard and a quizzical eyebrow.

'She's twelve,' Lennon answered for him, shaking his head slowly, features screwing up in mild disgust.

'Jesus!' said Harry, 'I always thought she was older than that, I mean she looks older.'

'Cheers, Harry, you're a great help, that makes me feel a lot better, but I'd prefer it if you didn't have designs on my daughter.'

'I never said that Dyl! I'm just saying she looks old for her age. I thought she was sixteen, y'know legal tender.'

Dylan turned to his brother, 'are you gonna punch him or am I?'

'Less of the legal tender talk, Hazza, alright? Dylan's depressed enough as it is.'

'What does Kirsty think of all this?' Harry steered the subject in a slightly different direction.

'She's just as pissed off as me, but she can't really say too much on the subject, she was pregnant at seventeen with Lucy, so we can't really lecture her on the subject can we?'

'Sure you can.' Harry gave a knowing smile. 'Just tell Lucy that you don't want her making the same mistakes that you two did . . .'

'You want me to tell my daughter that she was a mistake?'

'Well no, not exactly, but . . .' Harry defended himself.

'Hey, how's about we talk about something different, like errr . . . band names for example,' Lennon said, steering the conversation away. 'Okay, so far we were undecided between *Racist Baby, The Roadkill Puppeteers, Ded Sexy* and *Barry Bongo and the Bastards*? So what's it gonna be?'

Trust Lennon to save a conversation, thought Dylan. This is what he needed, a few pints with his brother and his best mate to take him away from the hell week he'd suffered; seventy odd hours on the road, clocking close to two-thousand miles delivering computer parts up and down the country. And when he got back home, his wife was in tears after a screaming match with his promiscuous twelve year old daughter; a letter that had been sent home from school, hand delivered by the Head Teacher, Mr Moor, detailing her behaviour with a fellow male pupil.

The letter now lay in shreds on the kitchen floor, torn to pieces by Lucy upon confrontation by her mother. Dylan never got a chance to read it; Kirsty however filled him in with all the gory details. Apparently, Lucy just wanted the boy to like her. How do you punish a child that does that? It was bound to happen at some point, but why did it have to happen at school, and while she was only twelve? Was it he that was the bad father? Sure he'd been working away a lot, but what could he do? They needed the money, and if the overtime was there, he had to take it. The recession meant that he had to work twenty percent longer to make the same wage he was earning three years ago. The increasing utility bills each month didn't help matters and the same went for the higher rate on the mortgage.

Now there was talk of downsizing and letting a few drivers go. Restructuring they called it. Dylan didn't need that. He dreaded telling Kirsty more bad news; she'd crumble. Their relationship was strained as it was. She was already off work with depression and had been for the past year. She'd chosen not to go down the medicated route, for the fear of being dulled by pills. Instead she tried to stick to a routine of a multi-vitamin and an omega 3 tablet with breakfast, followed by a one hour walk around Darlow woods that bordered the town. Dylan encouraged her to get out and socialise. He urged her to take a class, enrol on a course. Anything would do to get her out of the house. She tried, but any endeavour only lasted a few weeks before she got bored or anxious. She preferred housework when she was having a shut in day, cleaning became her religion and obsession. Dylan didn't mind this regime she put herself through. It kept her mind busy and the washing was always done.

Dylan loved her with all his heart and soul. But she was difficult to live with at the best of times. His wage just covered the mortgage and bills, so treats and luxuries were rare when your head was dipping below financial waters.

'How about *Nun Chuckers*?' Harry suggested, wiping an accumulation of frothy Guinness foam from his top lip, 'it would be a great album cover!'

'We chuck nuns?' Dylan pondered, trying to conjure the image in his mind.

Lennon piped up with excited wide eyes as an idea formed, 'how about *Nun Fuc . . .*'

'No!' Dylan and Harry cried out in unison, voices so loud their table neighbours turned to cast disparaging gazes their way.

'I'm all for a name that incites controversy, just not one that can't be mentioned on the radio,' Dylan reasoned. 'We've got to think forward as well as outwards.'

'What if we spell it with a pee-aitch? *Nun Phuckers*?' Lennon enunciated.

Harry and Dylan both shook their heads whilst hiding their smiles.

The fantasy talk of setting up a band steered Dylan's mind away from family life. Every Saturday night and some Tuesdays if he was home early enough, Lennon on guitar, Harry on drums and himself on bass, played in the garage connected to the side of his house. They had a few of their own songs under their belt and a few half-decent covers; all they needed was a name they could agree on.

Personally, Dylan liked *The Galivants,* but Harry dismissed it straight away, arguing that there were too many of **THE** bands out there in the mainstream; they needed something further out there; such as *Racist Baby.* Lennon's choice of *The Road Kill Puppeteers* only made it because Harry liked the shock value and imagery it conjured up. Lennon also fancied going down the electronica route with the group name *Techtronic Plates.* Harry dismissed the idea. They were a guitar band. He didn't want to fuck around with blinks, bleeps and a laptop, keep it simple with a gritty, bluesy wall of sound.

Three further pints of Guinness and Jameson chasers later, (that Dylan and Harry paid for; aside from his benefits, Lennon never had any evidence of disposable income; ever) they still were undecided on a decent band name. The discussion would continue at tomorrow night's band practice along with more beer and maybe a sneaky joint if Harry was feeling generous with the green.

Upon leaving *The Green Tree,* a heavy downpour greeted them from the darkened heavens. Dylan invited Harry back for a nightcap but he bravely refused. He had work in the morning and he couldn't turn down the time and a half overtime. Harry set off home by himself in a drunken wayward stumble, Lennon asked if he could crash on Dylan's sofa. Naturally he agreed, how could he, one of the most amicable guys around, turn his brother down, especially on a piss rainy night like this?

It was a short, hurried walk down Westfield Road, past the shops, the six weeks' worth of road works and the dark and empty school playing field back to Dylan's house. When they got there, Lennon ran his hand up the windscreen of Dylan's rusty white Vauxhall Corsa, soaking up the thick droplets of water; he flicked them down the back of his brothers' neck. Dylan was long used to his brother's playful attitude, so he simply swept his arm back across the roof of the car, sending a chilled plume of water into his brothers' face. As the horseplay continued down the driveway, neither of them noticed the old man waiting at the bus stop across the road; as still as a shop dummy, clothes soaked through to his cold, white, liver spotted skin. He'd been there an hour before they'd arrived home, having missed his last bus to the next village. Even when Dylan fumbled his jingling keys into the front door lock, pushed the handle down, and went inside, they didn't notice that the old man was staring straight at Dylan's house with stoic, blank faced wonder.

Only when they were in the living room, powering up the Play Station for a *Call of Duty* session and arranging fresh drinks to imbibe them gleefully into the early hours of Saturday morning, did Dylan notice the old man across the road. As he drew the curtains shut to black out the orange glister from the streetlights outside, Dylan pondered:

'*I wonder what time the last bus is?*'

'C'mon Dyldo. Time for an arse kicking!' Lennon called as he loaded a level.

Dylan drew the curtains. Blanking out the old man at the bus stop in the rain from his mind, who waited patiently outside, but gave no clue as to what exactly he was waiting for.

CRaSH, BanG, WaLLOP

Morning broke through a promise of clear skies, and as it did, a brilliant red glow from the east nurtured the sweet tweeting of birds and the blossoming of delicate flowers. What it signified for Dylan and Lennon however was the beginning of a black monster of a hangover. In the stillness of the early morning, a spider hurried across the carpet, back to his hidey place beneath the dust strewn television stand after a night of scuttling and scampering across tickled faces whilst their owners snored their way through oblivious, though deep sleep cycles.

Lennon had crashed out on the sofa as promised, arms tucked up tight against his chest. Dylan however had passed out on the floor; Play Station controller still grasped in one hand, GAME OVER had blazed in red screen burn for the past six hours. The remaining taste of whisky turned his stomach, a nudge to his gut turned it further.

His wife kicked him lightly in the stomach; he groaned.

'Suppose you'll be wanting a coffee?'

'Please,' Dylan said, cracking open one lid to eyeball the army of fluff that resided upon the surface of the carpet landscape and his wife's purple painted toenails.

'Coffee?' she asked Lennon.

'Yes,' only his lips moved, the rest of his body remained in a highly tuned form of meditation that dictated the less movement the better for his immediate health and well-being.

'What time did you get in?' Kirsty asked, still towering over the top of him. With eyes still half closed, she pulled the pink flowered dressing gown tight around her waist, tying the belt in a tight knot.

'Don't know, what time did the pub shut?' Dylan replied.

'You woke me about half one, you were cheering.'

'I think that was when we killed all of them Nazi Zombies; they had to die.'

'Two sugars... no . . . make it three,' Lennon said completely unrelated to the conversation, '. . . and bacon, bring me lots of bacon. I need me some burnt dead pig.'

Dylan turned his open eye up towards his towering wife, her blonde hair catching the glow through the curtains, making her just that little bit more beautiful in spite of his grating hangover.

'Christ on a bike! You look gorgeous this morning. Sorry if we woke you last night.'

'That's okay; I got straight back to sleep anyways.'

'Good, bacon butties stat!' Dylan gave a hopeful yet devilish smile directed at his wife.

'I'll see if we've got any bacon, Len you want one?'

'And eggs, scrambled . . . if you have any.'

'I'll see what I can rustle up. You wanna help me, darling?'

Dylan groaned, then pushed himself up from the living room carpet, spitting out flecks of dust and fluff from his mouth. His stomach felt like a listing ship, ready to capsize its alcoholic cargo should the going get too rough.

'If I have to . . .'

'You do.'

'How's our darling princess this morning?' Dylan asked as he unsteadily got to his feet, his voice buttered with sarcasm.

'Fine, far as I know. After you two had words, she bolted off to her room and stayed there all night. It was great; I could watch whatever I wanted on TV. Managed to watch three episodes of *Dexter,* so every cloud . . .' Kirsty smiled in that wary way of hers then turned round and opened the curtains. A burning wave of bright, white light from the Saturday morning flooded in, half blinding Dylan. Lennon squinted, screwing his face up into a wrinkled ball. He turned to face the back cushion of the sofa.

'Jesus wife! You trying to kill us? You know what light does to us when we're hung-over, we're like goddamned vampires. We'll burn up in a burst of flames!'

'Get over it you daft lug,' Kirsty motioned towards him and kissed him on the cheek, 'I'll try and find some meat for breakfast. Maybe you should brush your teeth?'

'Cheers, darling, you're so sweet.'

'Your breath smells like you've been tonguing Lennon's arse.'

'I didn't ask the Dyldo to do it,' Lennon added with a squinting smile, 'but I let him because he's my brother and I love him. I can't help his compulsions.'

'Hardy-ha!' Dylan mock laughed back.

Kirsty headed for the kitchen, in the space she left was the view across the road. The old man was still at the bus stop. Somehow, this strange sight sobered the bleary-eyed Dylan up, clicking on concern. He walked towards the window, trying to make some sense of the situation. Why would he still be there? He seemed to be in some sort of trance, he hadn't moved a muscle, unless this was one of Len's sick jokes. But not even Dylan could see the funny side of this bizarreness yet.

'Len, check this out.'

Lennon turned and opened an eye to see that his brother was gazing out of the bay window.

'Is it a bird; is she jogging? I'm not moving unless she's got great big tits.'

'I heard that!' Kirsty protested from the kitchen while she filled the kettle from the sink, 'ladies present!'

'Correction, I'm only moving if she's got better tits than Kirsty.'

'I heard that too!'

'You were meant to. Three sugars sweetness,' Lennon reminded her of his refreshment request.

'Len, get up and check this out,' Dylan urged.

Begrudged but bound by curiosity, Lennon peeled himself away from the sofa and with a weary stumble, joined his brother by the window.

'It's an old man waiting for a bus. Fucking great. You got me up for that. I need a piss now that I've moved. You broke the seal.'

'He was out there last night; he was waiting at the bus stop when we got back from *The Tree*.'

'You saying he stood out there in the rain all night?'

'I reckon.'

'Maybe it's that paedo who fancies you. We'll have to get you a wig.'

They both paused, fixing their gaze on the well-dressed old man across the road. His suit still looked damp and bedraggled from the evening's onslaught of heavy rain. Behind him lay the fence that bordered the school field. A group of young boys wearing a rainbow of varying footie shirts, joyfully played football in the freedom of the Saturday morning sun, sliding long tackles across the splendour of the damp grass. Dylan made a little bet with himself that they didn't have mortgage worries, or a sponger brother, or a wife that resented them for all the hours they worked or a twelve year old daughter that couldn't keep her hands off her boyfriend's . . . He derailed his train of thought from that track of worry and switched back to the task in hand.

'Is he staring at us?' Dylan finally asked.

'I think he might be. Maybe he's had a stroke.'

'And forgotten to collapse?'

'Viagra keeping him stiff and straight?' Lennon offered, 'medical technologies nowadays, eh?'

From the kitchen, Kirsty let out a startled scream that sliced straight down the centre of their hangovers like a chainsaw through ice cream.

Dylan and Lennon didn't waste any time in forgetting the old man across the road and the after effects of last night's boozing, rushing into the kitchen with a brief though troubled look of concern at each other, an urgent blast of adrenalin coursing through alcohol diluted capillaries.

Kirsty stood with her face caught in a frame of shock, mouth agape, gaze fixated on the window. One hand covered her mouth as if poised to catch the next shriek to escape her mouth. As soon as the two brothers entered the kitchen, she shook a shaking finger towards the kitchen window. They followed her invisible line and saw what had startled her.

Mrs Loughery, the delectable housewife from next door was standing in their back garden.

Stark-Bollock-Titty-Naked, as the day she was born, but with a good deal more feminine curves.

'Why's there a naked woman in your back garden?' Lennon asked, peering closer, half- admiring the fine figure of a woman, yet still half-frightened by the curious sight.

'I was kinda wondering that myself, Len.'

'She's wet,' Kirsty added.

'You can tell that from here?' Lennon questioned, concentrating his gaze on her crotch whilst fumbling in his pocket.

'No dumbo! I mean her skin. Look, her towel is on the grass, she must have just got out the shower.'

Kirsty was right, Mrs Loughery, despite being in her forties had a fine body. Droplets of water covered her upper body, her nipples proved hard with the cool freshness of the morning. Her silky brown hair laid slick and dark, like strands of succulent oil over the globes of her white shoulders. A white towel lay crumpled on the grass only a few feet away.

'You think she's had a stroke or something?' Kirsty pondered.

'I wouldn't mind a stroke.' Lennon said in his usual priapic manner. He had his phone in his hand and was gearing up to take a picture through the window. 'How come you've never introduced us Dyl?

'Shut up Len!' Kirsty scolded, slapping the phone down, 'this is serious; she might have had a breakdown or something. And put that damned phone away.'

Sheepish, Lennon did as he was told.

'Quiet you two! We should call the police or an ambulance or something,' Dylan put forward. He looked round for his phone after having dumped it somewhere in the kitchen last night.

'I've no credit,' Lennon announced, slipping his phone back into his pocket.

'Should we let her in, she'll catch her death out there,' Kirsty's face had gone pale, the blood drained away through as if the plug that held in her worry had been pulled.

'There's an old guy at the bus stop across the road as well,' Dylan mentioned.

'What's that got to do with anything? What's that got to do with Joy Loughery being crazy and naked in our back yard?'

'Dylan reckons he's been there since last night,' Lennon added.

Kirsty cast a quizzical look his way, as if to ask, *is that true?*

'He was there when we got back from the pub, he was there this morning. Weird huh?'

'Something's wrong. I don't know what, but something's wrong.' Kirsty said with a quiver in her voice. Dylan and Lennon both nodded in agreement, jaws stern, brows creased with concern. The joke was over now.

'What's wrong?' A tired little voice asked from the living room. The three adults span round half startled. Lucy was standing there dressed in her SpongeBob Square Pants pyjama's, her scowling face a picture of usual solemn moodiness, hair like a murdered mess of crows fighting over a bag of dead snakes and snapped twigs. Dylan imagined what she'd looked like if she shaved it all off, would she end up looking like a male hating lesbian because she despised her old man so much.

'Nothing's wrong sweetie. You sleep ok?' Kirsty asked.

'Yeah, a weird dream that's all, kept waking me up. Unless Dad was on the Play Station again,' she glowered all her menace at her father.

'You fancy some breakfast?' Kirsty asked in her sweet manner, deferring from the developing situation at hand, trying to appease her daughter in order to avoid any arguments. It was a nice day outside, why ruin it?

'Yeah, sure,' Lucy yawned as if the screaming fits from last night had never happened. Then her gaze fixed on the nude neighbour in the back garden staring straight back at her. Then she said as casually as ever, but clearly sobered by the sight. 'Why's Mrs Loughery in our back yard?'

'Don't forget *nekid*,' Lennon added with an oily little smile and horny eyes.

'Yeah, why hasn't she got any clothes on?'

'We don't know, Luce, we've only just seen her ourselves,' Dylan answered.

'I think you should call an ambulance,' Lucy added, moving closer to the window to get a better look at the strange sight that stared straight back at her.

'Should we? I mean nothing's really happened yet.' Kirsty questioned her daughter's common sense. Nobody answered, still dumbfounded by the unfolding situation. The procrastination wasn't solving anything, but they didn't want reprimanding for wasting the time of the emergency services either.

'Morning, Uncle Lenny,' Lucy chirped, 'how's the job hunt going?' Dylan detected a heavy hint of sarcasm in her tone. Bitch-Mode was officially on.

Lennon cast Dylan a disapproving glare. 'Going fine, but I told you my names Lennon, or Len if I like you. Don't call me Lenny.'

'Un I ten' da rabbits,' she mocked in a simple, semi-mongoloid tone.

'Lucy!' her mother chided with a scowl.

'Christ, Luce! I hate that impression, don't do it. It freaks me out!' Lennon bit back..

Dylan looked at his daughter, his brother, then back out at the nude neighbour in his garden. He ignored their petty dispute and said, 'What do we do? Our neighbour is naked in my back yard. Do I take her a blanket; let her come inside, what? She's clearly having some sort of breakdown. Thoughts people?'

'I know what I'd do,' Lennon grinned.

'Perve!' Lucy screwed her nose up at her uncle's comment, picked up a knife from the draining board and lunged at Lennon. He squeaked in protest and danced backwards into the dining table, pulling his gut in and curving his spine into a C-shape to avoid the flaying blade. Dylan intervened, grabbing his daughter's wrist and squeezed, bending her arm until she grimaced and let go of the blade. The butter knife dropped to the floor with a clatter. Blunt, but still, the intention to sever an artery was there.

Kirsty continued her disapproving scowl, picked the knife up at her daughter's feet, and dropped it in the sink.

'Hey, I was just playing!'

Dylan glared at his daughter and brother with a burrowing look that surprised them both. Dylan was usually a Zen like master of patience and acceptance. When he was pissed off, he meant business.

'Shut up you two, Lucy stop being a bitch, Len stop being a dick. With that freak at the bus stop, this is starting out to be a very weird morning.'

'What freak at the bus stop?' Lucy asked, her face furrowing into seriousness. She ceased her struggle against her father; he relented and let go of her thin wrist.

'There's an old guy across the road. He's being waiting at the bus stop since last night,' Dylan informed.

'In the rain,' Lennon added helpfully.

Lucy didn't respond, instead she padded into the living room and looked out the window at the old guy across the road. He too stared straight back at her. She watched him for a few seconds. The expression the old man pulled wasn't born of malice; it was just plain, as if he was bored with life or lost in a vacant daydream. That seemed to be the scariest thing, the fact that his expression didn't falter, didn't change, as if it had stuck with the changing of the breeze whilst caught in the grip of fugue. He didn't even seem to be breathing.

As Lucy watched the old man and the old man watched Lucy, a second stranger entered the stage of the front window. Across the road on the same side as the old man, a guy in his twenties, good looking, wearing a blue baseball cap stuck out at a hip-hop wannabe angle. In his hand was leash connected to a fluffy German Shepherd. As he approached the house, he slowed, whilst the eager dog tugged him forward on their usual morning route. She'd seen him before school, sometimes he jogged, and sometimes he had a girl with him. That made her a little bit jealous. She could imagine him taking her to the cinema or maybe grabbing a Maccy D's. The young guy's path faltered and he started to carve a desire line from the path and onto the grass, his gaze now fixated on Lucy. For some reason she smiled, transfixed on him as he was on her. Could he see her? Why would he look at her? The guy dragged the German Shepherd onto the road towards the house. The dog seemed bothered at this change of direction and halted his advance as best he could.

Tyres squealed like a stuck monster, then a blue estate car slammed into the young guy, his body arched, the cap flew away from his jarring, snapping head. The lead connecting him to the dog went deadly tight, pulling taut as the German Shepherd was forced in an opposite direction, a tight leather noose strangled around the dog's neck. The Shepherd gave a tumultuous yelp that was audible over the shriek of tyres grinding against wet tarmac. The young man tumbled over the top of the bonnet, transforming the windscreen into a sheet of broken snow before taking off the driver's side wing mirror then crashing down upon the hard, unforgiving tarmac, as the car squealed to a stop. Lucy grasped at her mouth that gaped in shock, anything to stifle the scream that wanted to escape her lips.

Her mother turned from the kitchen, her eyes rapidly digesting the aftermath of what had occurred outside, refusing to believe what they saw. The young man lay sprawled on the tarmac, legs twisted awkwardly in competing directions, the dog now slack and still on the end of the lead, its neck no doubt broken.

Dylan and Lennon burst from out of the kitchen, temporarily forgetting about the nude Mrs Loughery in the garden. At the front window they eyed the scene of carnage with a bizarre sense of wonder. Dylan didn't think anymore. He acted. Shoeless and sockless he bounded out of the front door, Lennon followed suit.

Now deciding that the time was right, Kirsty picked up her mobile and dialled 999, her purple painted toes hurried her to the front door to check on the unfolding situation.

The driver of the car had gotten out the vehicle with his hands on his head, his head shaking in disbelief as he tried to grasp what had just happened just before his head snapped up and looked past Dylan with glaring eyes. Dylan ignored him and focused on the young victim that lay bloody and twisted on the kerb side like a blood-filled bag of limbs. A young couple also taking their dog for an early morning walk stopped to gawp at the scene of the accident from the opposite side of the road.

Dylan stopped. A cloud of unease settled over him. He branched out his arm and caught Lennon by his collar as he passed, holding him back from venturing any further. Lennon's feet carried on Looney Tunes like until he was pulled back by his brother's fear led grip.

'Wait!' he hissed.

Dylan turned, Kirsty waited within the safety of the front door, waiting to see what happened next. She had one hand over the top of Lucy's shoulder, squeezing tight and secure. Her other hand held the phone to her ear; she was talking to someone, nodding even though the person on the other end of the line couldn't see her movement. An emergency operator he guessed.

'Don't go any closer.'

'Why?' Lennon questioned, bizarrely eager to help the injured. Sometimes he wanted to play hero, just in case some fit lass was watching and he'd have the chance to impress.

'Look at them.'

The young couple with the dog.

The once distraught driver.

The old man at the bus stop.

The gang of kids on the field.

Even the bent and twisted young lad smeared across the tarmac outside his house, bubbles of blood blew from his nose as the breath left his punctured lungs, eyes fixed wide, yet remaining as calm as a stoned Buddha, despite his probable broken spine and multiple fractures.

All of them were staring blankly at the house.

A tickle down his spine corralled the hairs on his neck to prick up; a primeval alarm within him sensed danger, in the very least, unease. Something was rotten on Westfield Road.

With his fingers still wrapped tightly around the scruff of his brother's neck, Dylan retreated towards the relative safety of the house. Not before they both noticed that standing beside the garage only a few feet further down the drive, was a jogger in day-glo shorts and vest, along with Mrs Loughery's husband Mike and their three-year-old daughter, Lexi. This added an additional three more Starers, gazing blankly at the brickwork on the side of the garage, adding to the growing group that now inhabited Westfield Road.

THE GaTHERING CROWD

'Who do we call this time? The police? Another ambulance? Christ is that guy dead?' Kirsty asked as she hurried her shocked husband and brother-in-law into the house. She locked the door behind her and urged them all into the living room. With her mobile clasped tightly in her hand, she stared at the phone feeling she didn't recognize the useless object. She'd already rung up for one ambulance, what good would ringing 999 again do?

Lennon ran his fingers through his hair in an attempt to distress what he just had seen. His fingers gripped, then tugged, pulling at the strands, as if this would somehow tighten and reaffirm his slickening grip on reality.

'The guy with the dog?' Lucy asked solemnly, 'he's still watching us. Why?'

Dylan noticed his daughter's lip tighten when she said dog, she didn't mention that he'd been hit by a car, it didn't need to be said. They all knew who she was talking about.

Dylan moved to her, grabbed her and held her close, 'don't look Luce, you don't need to look a...'

Lucy pushed her father away with a curling scowl and the length of her arms, breaking the embrace before breaking his heart.

'This changes nothing! You were a dick last night; I should be able to see who I want!'

Dylan bit his lip and cooled his voice before he exploded, he looked at his wife for some kind of support or backup, but the spectators outside the window entranced her, as it did Lennon.

'Lucy, you're twelve. You can't act like...'

'I'm thirteen, Dad! You missed my birthday remember? Oh that's right, you forgot!'

'Luce, I'm sorry, I was working. . .'

Lucy muttered a string of expletives and stormed into the kitchen. The last word he could make out was '...coffee...'

'Isn't she a bit young to be drinking coffee?' Dylan asked of his wife.

'She a bit young for many things Dyl, but she does them anyway. That's part of growing up,' Kirsty replied. She didn't even turn away from the window. 'She's at that awkward in-betweener stage now.'

'Well, have you had the talk about it with her, y'know? The boys and bees and all that.'

'Woah,' Lennon protested and turned to his brother, 'Should we really be talking about that stuff now, I don't want to hear about tampon tantrums. I thought we were calling another ambulance or the cops or some shit.'

'Too late,' said Kirsty. Her gaze shifted up the road. 'They're here.'

Dylan turned his attention back to the bay window and looked out. An ambulance slowed as it approached the accident, drawing close, the lights flashed once and then it stopped outside the house. Two green uniformed paramedics stepped out of the ambulance; both took one look at the scene of carnage then started to walk down the drive, ignoring the bent and crumpled dog walker that lay smeared and torn open on the road. The paramedics stepped through his blood, approached the door, stood in front of it, and did nothing. Quizzically, Dylan moved into the hall. Through the frosted glass, he could make out two green, man shapes. They didn't knock.

They didn't ring the bell.

They did nothing.

With an uneasy quiet, they stood behind the frosted pane, becoming another part of the ominous crowd that had started to congregate outside Dylan Keene's home.

'Are they just standing there?' Kirsty whispered.

Dylan nodded. Fear paralysing every other muscle.

'Will they send more paramedics?' Lennon asked.

'Eventually, if these don't call back to headquarters, more will come,' Dylan left the hall, closing the door behind him and returned to the living room. Lennon followed. He could smell coffee. Somehow, it felt wrong to want something nice, hot and refreshing.

'I was afraid you'd say that. We should start charging them admission,' Lennon tried to joke. No one laughed.

Dylan moved towards the bay window to ponder. He could see the two new additions beneath the porch roof, the paramedics stood side by side at his front door. He could see the couple with the dog, staring blankly at the house. Though strangely, it felt like they were looking through him. The distraught driver had soon forgot about the man and dog he had run over, standing over the still staring body of the bloodied and bent young man, they both appeared to be staring at the house. The young man on the floor appeared to be so still that Dylan couldn't tell whether he was dead or alive. Either way, his eyes were wide open and he was looking at the house. The kids across the road on the school field looked this way as well. Six of them as still as Gormley figures in the distance, staring in his direction all the same.

He couldn't see Mr Loughery or Lexi Loughery, or the random jogger; the three of them were still tucked around the side of the house. Dylan knew they were still there.

'Must be infection or mass delirium,' Dylan deduced, 'maybe something in the water . . . , Christ, tell Lucy not to drink the water! Lucy!'

Kirsty's eyes bulged wide as she ran for the kitchen, 'Luce you heard your dad, don't drink the water!'

'Whatever.' Dylan could only hear his daughter's stroppy attitude tinged voice as a wall separated them. Metaphorically and physically.

Lennon joined his brother by the window.

'What d'ya think Sherlock? What's caused this?' Lennon asked, smiling much more than the situation dictated. Dylan didn't mind that Lennon was always smiling for some reason or another. He had no worries. No commitments. A free agent. No mortgage. No income tax. No VAT. No money back, no guarantee. Somehow, he envied his unshackled, wandering nature. Lennon Keene was a relentless shyster and a sofa crashing layabout who fumbled from one situation to the next without much thought for the dire consequences. Like a big eyed, wag tailed puppy in a china shop. He guessed it was the constant flow of weed in his system that fuelled his happy-go-lucky nature and cushioned him from reality.

'Mass hysteria, without the hysteria, poison gas cloud, bad signal from mobile telephones frying people's brains? Christ, who knows?' Dylan let the pondering loose, a wounded beast that had no cure.

'Someone does, we just have to figure out who.'

'Brother,' Dylan slapped a hand on Lennon's shoulder, 'that may be the smartest thing you've ever said.'

'Do I get a sticker?'

'You get to stay another hour, good enough?'

'Hardy ha! I ain't going nowhere bruv.'

They both sighed as the town bus that passed by the house roughly every forty minutes from 6:11am onwards, pulled up across the road, blocking out the old man at the bus stop who had stood in the rain.

The bus, which was half filled with OAP's on-route to run errands in town and students who hadn't passed their driving tests, was a collage of faces, each of which turned round in unison and stared directly and casually at the house. The driver stalled the bus with a gentle jolt, He turned toward the house, following the gaze of his passengers.

Dylan shivered.

Kirsty stepped into the living room and handed them both a glass of orange juice. Dylan and his brother both sipped the cool, tangy liquid sunshine whilst contemplating the situation that was unfolding outside. The citric acid cut through the clag that had formed in their mouth since last night's session.

'So we can't drink the water then?' Kirsty whispered.

'I wouldn't. Not until we know what's going on, there could be anything in it.'

'Should we bottle some up. Y'know just in case?' Kirsty asked.

'That might not be such a bad idea. Preserve what we can…'

'While we can,' she finished the sentence for him. They smiled at each other.

'It's a flash mob, it must be. Some kids have organised it on Face Space or something? Maybe they'll start dancing in a bit.' Lennon theorised, nodding to himself, 'yeah?'

'No,' Dylan responded. Lennon's forehead furrowed. 'One, why would they invite old people, and two, there's a guy out there who got smashed by a car and nobody seems to be doing a damned thing about it. Even flash mobs gotta have a heart somewhere.'

'True. Good point. Duly noted,' Lennon returned to sipping his juice, pondering further.

'We should fill up every container we can find with water. We've got a few empty bottles under the sink, we'll fill every pan, every cup, the bath, every old takeaway container we can find. Before this gets worse.'

'Why?' asked Lennon.

'Well, we don't know how long this'll last, do we?'

'It'll be over by this afternoon, tonight the latest. Everything is temporary.'

Dylan gave his brother a glaring look. 'Like the water supply?'

'Again, good point. I retract my statement.'

'I'll get started on that, why don't you check the news, see if there's anything related to what's going on outside,' Kirsty left for the kitchen. Pots and pans rattled, water gushed intermittently from the faucet.

Dylan turned on the television whilst Lennon continued staring outside the front window, straight back at the Starers.

The news was usual and boring. A footballer cheated on his wife; again. More deaths during a violent protest in the war ravaged Middle East. An earthquake in the Atlantic puts the west coast of Africa on a tsunami warning. A hurricane in the States kills fifty in the Florida Keys, the usual crap. But nothing about what was going on outside. It must be local.

The newscaster staring straight at him unnerved Dylan a bit. He thumbed the red button and turned off the television. He didn't want to be stared at anymore. He'd check the news in half an hour or so.

Dylan headed back into the kitchen. Kirsty was at the sink filling the large pan she usually used for boiling spaghetti while his daughter sat down at the table nursing a glass of orange juice, gazing blankly at the wall.

'It's just us,' Dylan told her, 'It's a local job. Nowhere else is experiencing the same weirdness as us.'

Kirsty stopped filling the heavy pan and placed it on the worktop. 'Strange. It's giving me a bad feeling, the fact that they just stand there. It's like they're all waiting for something to happen. Poised.'

'Waiting for us to come out so they can eat our *brains.*' his mock zombie voice did nothing to raise even a smile from his wife.

'I think if the crowd harboured any hatred or hunger towards us they would have attacked the house already, don't you reckon?'

'Possibly.' Dylan drained his juice with a long gulp and placed the dirty glass on the counter top beside the sink.

'*Hey,* you gonna wash that up?' Kirsty questioned with a raised eyebrow.

'I don't think we can afford to waste the water, darling,' Dylan responded with a grin. He even managed a comforting rub of her bum while their daughter had her back to them.

'Hmmm . . . any excuse,' Kirsty whispered. She turned from the sink and embraced him, giving him a comforting peck on the cheek.

'I think that guy's dead out there,' Lennon called from the window.

Kirsty followed Dylan into the living room. Even Lucy showed concern and left the table to join them at the window. All four of them looked out at the circus of people gathering outside. The young guy with the dead dog lay on the road, legs twisted round awkward and misshapen, a shining puddle of dark blood formed around the tarmac beneath him. His eyes were open, still staring at the house. But he was dead; life had left his eyes despite them still being fixated on the house, his head now rested in broken peace on the kerbside. More strangers had gathered outside. Now well over fifty, all spaced out, in mind as well as location. Scattered was the word Dylan was looking for, they were scattered.

A policeman.

A lady with twins in a silver cross, the toddlers looked over the side of the pram, dummies still in their mouths, both mirroring each other's placid, cherubic gaze.

A cyclist had stopped, now he leant on one leg whilst still sat on his bike, his gaze fixed earnest and unrelenting upon the house.

He didn't recognize anybody he knew. All strangers. They didn't live in the largest of towns, but it was impossible to know everybody nowadays.

'This is getting weird,' Lennon said with a shake of his head.

'You're saying that now?' Kirsty managed half a broken smile.

'Yeah, it's starting to sink in that we've woken up in the Twilight Zone.'

'It looks that way, brother,' Dylan replied.

'You guys mind if I smoke?' Lennon asked; his voice went high when he found himself under stress. He sounded like a trumpet blown by a baboon. He searched round anxiously for his cigarettes, patting his pockets down, his face grimacing in disappointment. Lennon then headed over to his jacket that he'd slung over the back of the sofa.

'Not in the house,' Kirsty warned, 'I hate the smell.'

'Bathroom window mate,' Dylan pointed upstairs, he didn't smoke in front of his wife, not since he'd told her that he'd quit. She thought it was a waste of money; which it was. Dylan went to great effort to hide his secret habit; only smoking outside so the odour didn't penetrate his clothes, washing his hands after each cigarette and chewing gum to take the taste of ash from his breath.

Lennon left and headed upstairs. A brief worry materialized that he might let in whatever was causing the weirdness outside. But if it wanted to get in, it would be inside already. Dylan shrugged the thought off and turned the television back on in time for the local news.

Kirsty and Lucy continued to gawp at the Starers outside. Transfixed by the mass that had accumulated outside their house; even as they watched, ten more people joined the crowd. Animals it seemed, were unaffected by what was going on as a stray Labrador roamed the crowd, sniffing each individual's shoes with weary interest. Oddly, the dog's tail was tucked firmly between its legs as it investigated the crowd. Sulking at their feet, a worry pained the canine.

The local news brought up little of interest as the female newscaster droned on about local events; a twenty-year-old goldfish that had died and an up and coming rock band made up of eleven year olds. Dylan was about to turn off when halfway through handing over to the weather girl, the female newscaster stood up and left the screen without explanation, noisily dropping her notes all over the desktop in the process. The camera remained fixed on the empty chair and the desk of scattered papers.

A spike of ice split Dylan Keene's spine in two as he shivered from the image on screen. This wasn't right.

'Girls,' Dylan said, his voice on the verge of breaking down. They both turned round from the window, 'I think it's spreading. The local television studio is what . . . Ten miles from here?'

Lucy and her mother turned round and looked at the empty studio on the screen. They watched as it remained that way for three minutes before a message scrawled across a blue-sky background appeared and said:

We are experiencing a technical difficulty.
Normal programming will return shortly.

Even after Lennon returned downstairs from his fourth cigarette, the screen remained the same. Dylan got the feeling they weren't coming back, so he turned off the television and begrudgingly let the cloud of worry that was forming around his mind grow just that little bit bigger.

Suffocation

Lennon paced, maybe for an hour or so. Back and forth, back and forth from the bay window to the kitchen.

Back and forth.

Back and forth.

Forth and back.

Forth and back.

Soon his ambling repetition had carved out a vague desire line into the beige carpet. He hungered for a cigarette but he'd already smoked his last four within the space of an hour out of the bathroom window. He had a perve over Mrs Loughery from above, but he gained no pleasure from knowing she was completely out of her mind. An obese elderly woman had appeared in the back garden. She stood three feet behind Mrs Loughery, except she had a bright pink dressing gown on, covering her no doubt grotesque flabby curves. *Thank Christ*, thought Lennon.

***

Curled up by the bay window, Lucy stared outside. At first she had been unmoved by the unfolding strangeness of the day, but now, whilst everyone around her fretted and worried, the reality of the situation had dawned on her. She had tried to put it down to shock, her carrying on as if it were just a normal Saturday; get up, bitch at dad while she ate breakfast, bitch at dad until he gave her a lift into town.

Bitch, bitch, bitch.

Every Saturday she'd head into town with Poppy Smith, Whitney King and Sammi Knowles. She was head of their little clique, whatever she said, went. If she wanted to see a film, they'd all go see a film. If she wanted to go shopping, they'd all go shopping. They just agreed with her. It was a gift.

Or maybe she was just a bitch.

With her ever so poor grades at school, bitching at people was the only thing she was good at really.

Vicky Hartlet from school once said she should take a G.S.C.E in Cow. She'd easily get an A+*. She pulled Vicky Hartlet down to her knees by her hair that day and pulled her through a muddy puddle. She'd never told anyone, neither of them had. Her parents knew she could be a bitch, but they weren't privy to the full extent of her irritable ways. It was in her nature, it was a struggle to be nice sometimes.

Bitch, bitch, bitch.

She repeated it to herself in her head.

She'd seen a man get run over. And she wanted to carry on as normal.

Christ, she was such a bitch, why couldn't she just react like a normal person? She heard her mum and dad talking a few nights back about how she might have ADHD and asparagus syndrome or something like that.

Maybe she should give her dad a hug. Today seemed liked the kind of day he'd need it, families should stick together, right? She'd heard him the other day saying that he was having a bad time at work.

Should she change because the situation dictated it?

No, he had enough going on with the people outside. She'd leave it, talk to him later when the people go away. If they go away, she hoped.

She looked over at her mum and smiled. Kirsty Keene tried to smile back, but Lucy didn't believe it. Mum was faking it.

Lucy shivered as a tiny ghost danced down her back with icy tiptoes.

A sense of déjà vu settled over her. She'd felt the same when she saw the man get run over. She put it down to tiredness. Blame the dream.

Parts of it came back to her. Flashes, scenes, half-spoken sentences lost to the abyss of sleepy thoughts.

The man getting run over.

Her mother's fake smile.

The man in the coat.

An ache in the pit of her belly, a sense of straining fullness that burned her insides like acid as it pressed against her.

That was all she could remember. Just flashes, a sense of the scene, nothing more. She had definitely dreamt about today last night.

It frustrated her.

But not the man in the coat, he outright scared her. He was what woke her up so urgently. His smile gave her a shiver of cold dread. She hoped that she didn't have to dream about him again.

***

Kirsty Keene had grown irritated at her brother-in-law's pacing about five minutes in. That was over an hour ago. She felt right to not say anything as she didn't want to come across as a nag, and the situation had put enough stress on them already. Even now, she still wasn't sure what was going on.

It started like any other day, she mused to herself. Arguments, a drunken husband, and her late period had her bound up with enough worry. She was going to tell Dylan today, soon as Lennon had left and Kirsty had vanished off to her friends. She'd bought a pregnancy testing kit, she just hadn't the guts to use it yet. She wanted Dylan beside her when they found out. When she found out about Lucy, he hadn't been there. He'd been working late as usual, stuck on some desolate road in the middle of nowhere trying to find his destination. But it had been her fault, she could have waited but her impatience had got the better of her and she peed on the stick without him and regretted it ever since. It wasn't something couples did often, finding out they were to have a child together. But this time she would make sure that Dylan was with her to share the joy. When eventually she told him about being pregnant with Lucy, he got down on one knee and proposed straight away, saying that it was the right thing to do. He sold his car and she pawned some of her grandmother's jewellery that she'd been bequeathed, scraping together enough money and put a healthy deposit down on the house. The rest was hard-earned history.

Now it had led them all up to this extraordinary point in their lives with a strange crowd of people outside their home. Not battling hoards hungry for flesh like Dylan and Lennon's dumb zombie films, smashing windows and battering down doors to eat their succulent brain jelly. Just a crowd, absent of free thought and expression, strangely hypnotised by the house and its occupants. For whatever reason, Kirsty didn't like the way this was going to end. There had already been a death and it wasn't even nine o'clock in the morning. The caring nature of society expected that they go outside and help the poor lad who had been run down; but an unnerving sense of concern, something that whispered it was somewhat dangerous outside; they should stay where they were. She followed her gut, not her head, and not her heart. Her gut, that primeval membrane which forces us to flee any apparent dangers we sense in certain situations. Even when we could be brave, the gut is always right. They'd left the boy to die to guarantee their own safety.

She looked at her husband. Dylan stared out the window, his stance thoughtful and frozen, mirroring that of the Starers outside. Except Dylan blinked, she had noticed that none of them blinked. Had anyone else noticed this? Kirsty sidled up to Dylan and held his hand. It was cold and damp with sweat. He turned and smiled. She knew he didn't mean it.

***

Dylan had taken his wife's hand out of habit. In reality, he wanted to run, get in the car and just *go*. If they made it, well good for them.

You selfish bastard, he told himself. You can't leave them, they're your family. They might bicker and annoy the hell out of you but as the alpha male in this pack, it's your job to protect them.

I know.

Even in an absent-minded manner, he nodded in agreement with himself. Protect the family. Besides, who said outside was safer than inside. Nobody, because everybody he cared about was in this house, and they had no more of a clue of what was happening today than he did. The only people to know anything about what was going on were the people outside. And they were remaining rather tight lipped on the subject.

Dylan reached down, picked up the house phone, and dialled 999. Pressing the speaker to his ear, he heard the phone at the other end just ring and ring.

'Are you trying the police again?' Kirsty asked.

'Yeah.'

'Anybody answering?'

Dylan turned off the phone after twenty or so impatient rings and replaced it back in its holster. 'What do you think?' he responded with a grim intention.

Lucy's laptop sat on the kitchen table, even though he'd told her a thousand times not to leave it there enticing burglars to break in.

Dylan tapped a few keys and the screen glowed to life. He clicked Internet Explorer, first checking the news, which revealed nothing new since yesterday. He quickly fired off a group email to a few friends, both asking for their help and warning them not to come near the house as something strange was going on. He couldn't say anymore as he didn't know any better. Disappointed, Dylan closed the laptop down. It seemed the world didn't care or just didn't know about their predicament.

'What do we do now?'

'Will you stop asking questions?' Dylan snapped, making Kirsty jump back. 'Christ woman, d'ya think I've got the answers? Do you really think I can come up with a solution? To this?' he swept his hand wide, indicating to the Starers beyond the bay window, 'to them outside? How? What can I do?'

'Dylan…, I'm scared. That's all. I just need some reassurance that everything is… gonna be okay.' Kirsty's face crumbled into a distraught, teary mess. She turned heel and ran upstairs. Dylan cursed and ran after her.

***

Lennon and Lucy looked at each other, and then back outside.

'What do you think happened?' Lucy asked as a strange lady dressed only in her underwear casually walked up to the house and stopped on the lawn; again, like the others, the lady stared at the house with the same vacant expression. A hairy man with a protruding potbelly, nude except for a pair of flip-flops and a heavy gold chain around his neck stood proudly next to the stalled bus, kindly balancing out the male-to-female nudity ratio.

'Bath salts probably. Or maybe a military experiment gone wrong,' Lennon theorised firmly, settling his elbows on the windowsill, trying to out stare the new arrival. He lost.

'Must be some kinda nerve agent. Incapacitates the victim, renders them dumb, easier to make them surrender. You could take over any country without firing a bullet or bomb. What's your theory?'

'I don't know, it's like the end of the world,' she half whimpered through tightened lips, 'I expected it to have a bigger bang. Y'know, a meteorite or nuclear bomb maybe.'

'So what do you think? What's your take?'

Lucy narrowed her eyes as if pondering some great equation; then, 'I had a dream last night, it was weird. Like I've seen this before.'

'In your dream?'

'Yeah.'

'It's déjà vu, that's all.'

'Nah,' she dismissed, 'I dreamt everything: These people, my mum's fake smile and the guy getting hit by the car. All these blank faces. Everything.' In fact, the more she thought about it the more she remembered. Though not in the order it was happening.

Fingers breaking against aged rocks in the soil.

Buckets of water.

Cold beans.

Fire in the darkness, faraway, but too close.

Blood on the windows.

Screams curdling the night air.

The Ache.

'Déjà vu is just a process of the brain, like a computer running a system check. It makes you think you've experienced something before, whereas it's just a similar object or place or situation that triggers the feeling.'

'Is that your theory?'

'Sort of,' Lennon answered, 'Wikipedia. I got side-tracked whilst researching some song lyrics.'

'Well . . . what I dreamt was this, it was déjà vu over and over again. More than once. Not just a moment, but an event, like a full movie I had seen, not just snap shots.'

'Okay then Psychic Sally. What happens next?'

'I don't know, but the last thing I remember is a man.'

'Oh yeah, a boy from school. Or a teacher this time.'

'Shut up, Len.'

'I'm kidding. Sorry. What does this dream guy look like?'

'I don't know. I can see him but I can't really describe him. He's white but sorta tanned. Good looking like a film star or something. He looks like he could be famous, but at the same time he could just fit into the crowd like an everyday bloke.'

'This crowd?' Lennon pointed to the mass of people outside. 'Your description doesn't help us much. I mean what was he wearing?'

'I think he was wearing a coat,' Lucy replied with a glum croak, 'a coat made of skin. I think it's human skin.'

And that silenced Lennon. He stared back outside, dreading whatever came next.

***

Kirsty had been a Goth the week Dylan had also dipped his toe in those black eye-liner waters. Her blonde hair had been stained raven black during her teenage years, as was Dylan's brown, greasy mop. That had been how they'd met, through similar circles of friends, same interests and they both liked the same music. Whilst Dylan wore black to fit in with a crowd he hoped would accept him, Kirsty wore it because it made her feel better, somehow the allure of black made her dark world brighter. Having lost her father when she was ten, Kirsty hadn't seen much point in revelling in any joy in the world; in fact she thought she didn't deserve any happiness. As the years passed by, they got closer and closer. Apart from one brief spell where Dylan had a girlfriend, they'd been childhood sweethearts. And when Kirsty fell pregnant, she soon forgot about the darkness that haunted her, she had her own impending family to be concerned about. She didn't have time for fashionable depression; life was moving on and sweeping her along with it.

Though despite her now grounded nature, Kirsty was sometimes prone to going off into the deep end when some form of disaster struck the Keene household. The Corsa failing its MOT was followed by a fit of tears, an electric bill she'd have to ring up and split because they couldn't afford the full amount, Dylan had to dial the number and tell her not to be a baby about it. Whilst Dylan enjoyed being the less mature and least responsible in the relationship, sometimes he had to step up to the plate and take charge when she couldn't contain herself. Her overreactions to some situations were sometimes not the healthiest response; today being one of them.

'I'm sorry darling; this situation is just getting to me. It's getting to everybody.'

Kirsty nodded, nuzzling into her husband's chest, staining his t-shirt with dampened Rorschach blots.

'I mean look at Len,' Dylan continued, 'I don't know how he's gonna cope when his system is depleted of nicotine. He's been smoking since he was twelve . . . months.'

Kirsty managed a weak smile, a slight laugh, but still Dylan could see that the situation outside and inside was getting to her.

Their bed squeaked as she shifted her weight, cuddling deeper into his warmth.

'It's just so bizarre. Why us? Why now?' her voice went so high Dylan thought it sounded like it would break.

'Why not, it's got to happen to somebody, why not us?' Dylan reasoned.

'I suppose. I just can't figure it out. They scare me. I know they haven't hurt us or tried to get inside the house. But still...'

'Would you rather be one of them, or one of us? I prefer being inside.'

'God no!'

'Let's just see it as an adventure; try not to get on each other's nerves. Stick it out, see what happens.'

Kirsty pulled away and smiled at her husband, still smiling she said, 'what if they try to get in?'

Dylan moved his hands up to her face and pressed his thumbs into her forehead, and started to rub in slow, circular motions. Kirsty closed her eyes and groaned as the moment of stress melted away beneath his touch, her shoulders slumped and she fell into him, chin on his chest.

'We'll deal with that if it happens,' Dylan said in a delicate, soothing tone, running both thumbs up the centre of his wife's forehead, his index fingers crept towards her temples, aiding the relaxing motions.

'Shouldn't we be making spears or something, y'know getting ready to defend our home?' she said lazily.

'If it makes you feel better, we can do that.'

She smiled, 'strangely; I think it would.'

'You wanna spend the day making weapons? Like Rambo?'

'Not just weapons. I've got the horrible feeling that this isn't going to be over anytime soon.'

'How would you know that?'

'Just an unlucky guess.'

Dylan smiled this time.

'I don't think it's the water.'

'I think you're right,' Kirsty replied, pushing away his tenderising hands, cuddling back into the warmth that her husband offered.

Outside and high above, Dylan's ears attuned to a dreaded sound that only a rare percentage of the planet's ears ever hear.

Instinct told them both to look up at the ceiling as the drone squealed harder and closer by the second. He imagined a giant steel pterodactyl zoning in and screeching as it poised its talons ready to tear the roof from the house, plucking them out to grind and mash their salty flesh and bones to a still squirming meal.

It was the sound of a passenger jet in free-fall, droning violently, the pitch increasing towards a deadly crescendo as it neared the ground, piling on more velocity as gravity grabbed hold, never failing to relinquish its stubborn grip. The reverberation got louder and he hugged his wife tighter, praying to whatever god was left that it was only a cargo plane, two pilots tops. Not rows of dumb downed holidaymakers wandering aimlessly about the cabin in search of a house on Westfield Road they'd never find.

Please don't hit the house.
Please don't hit the house.
Please don't hit the house.

A pocket of air boomed against the house causing the windows to thump inwards but not to shatter. The entire building shook with the impact as metal met soil and jet fuel met the open air and a million blinking sparks. A mushrooming cloud of bright, bright light exploded out on the playing field. The plane had come down that fast and that sudden; they hadn't even seen it hit the ground. By the time their minds had processed what they had just witnessed, the fireball had grown to an immense size, dwarfing the house beneath its yellow shadow; a giant emerging beast from the brittle earth. The resulting pressure wave had knocked down the nearest gathered crowd in dumb droves. Some managed to stand back up, those closest to the flaming crater still awash with the falling gush of hungry orange fire. They didn't seem to care; they just stood burning away, dark chess pieces hiding amongst the awful light, a raging hot ball stirring up a melting soup of souls. Chunks of blackened and twisted metal erupted from the inferno, spiralling into the air and cart wheeling across the grass, towards the house. A few large pieces of shrapnel hit some of the bystanders, but nothing too large hit the house. A policeman took a hit to the back of the neck, the razor sharp sheet of metal cleanly taking the helmeted head completely off.

The decapitated body slumped to the ground with an urgent spurt of blood that became the profile of a black geyser in front of the flames. They heard the odd, tinny clunk of a bolt or rivet rain down upon the roof, cracking the odd tile. Apart from that, structurally they'd been lucky despite their proximity. The fireball punched higher up into the sky and then collapsed in on itself, falling down into its own crater. It felt like an eternity, but what they'd just seen had been over in seconds, barely a blink. A new monster was born of the inferno; black, bloated and towering, a domineering presence that carried what was left of the vacant dead up towards the empty heavens.

Don't look. It will depress the hell out of you and make this day far, far worse than it already is . . .

He stroked Kirsty's hair, wiped a tear from her eye and said, 'don't try to think about them, it will only make it worse.'

Kirsty started crying again, Dylan joined her as the stress that he had thought he'd vanquished came flooding back in droves. They sat for a while just holding each other as tight as they could without hurting one another.

***

When they returned downstairs, Lennon just looked at them and asked 'plane?' A silence fell between their eyes as the unimaginable had happened, plaguing their every thought. Mass death on their doorstep and not a damned thing they could do about it.

With wide eyes ready to cry, Dylan shook his head looked to the floor in disbelief. He couldn't look.

Although it was all they could think about, there seemed no good reason to speak of it. So they didn't. They couldn't even begin to comprehend the burning bloodshed outside their front door.

A consuming numbness swept through the house, silencing them whilst they watched the playing field burn. There was nothing they could have done. The flames continued to burn. They were rubbernecking. Dylan remembered back to a co-driver named Whitworth he once had a run out with, reminding him of every human's obsession with the vision of death. They were passing a bad smash-up involving a coach and a lorry on the other side of the motorway and naturally, every car was slowing down so the gore fiends could gawp in the hope of spotting a severed arm or a pile of entrails; sadly they were all satisfied. A body had fallen from the front end of the coach as it veered up the embankment and tipped over; smearing what was left of a human along the hard shoulder.

"I'll take the pictures, you count the dead," Whitworth had said, his eyes fixed on the scene of destruction as they ambled past.

You can't count the dead here, Dylan thought. The pyre was a human jigsaw of ashes, DNA and melted metal attachments such as fillings and false hips.

The oh-so-wrong stench of charred flesh filled their noses as the breeze leant the hungry inferno towards them, disturbing each of them on some deep primal level, ticking off alarmed sensors in their brain. That smell meant death. And somehow, they all knew it was coming for them.

***

A grim survival instinct took over and they all spent the day filling up every available container they had, whilst ignoring the scene of devastation outside. The mental blinkers did nothing to block out the smell that permeated every pore of their being. It was a smell their senses had never experienced before.

Burning human flesh.

When Dylan and Lennon had their parents cremated, they suffered no effects such as this one. The stench was ghastly, evil even, bringing a sense of a grisly war to the whole situation.

This is what Auschwitz must have smelt like, maybe even Ground Zero, not many Septembers ago, Dylan thought. Souls lost to dust.

They continued in earnest with their task, anything to take their minds off the scene of death outside the living room window. A few times Kirsty started crying without any provocation. Then she'd clench her jaw and fight back the tears for dead strangers and the worry of her own mortality.

Cups and mugs, pans and saucers. Even their collection of hot water bottles and thermos flasks were utilised. Lucy helped her mother with this in the kitchen, gently placing pan after pan after mug after cup on the table and worktops. She didn't mention anything of her premonition to her mother as she knew it would only upset her more.

Dylan cleaned the bath out and filled it to the brim with cold water, as he'd seen disaster experts do on a documentary he'd watched on worst case scenario survival. Immediately he felt better.

They would use the bath water for washing and flushing the toilet, topping it up as long as they had running water. They had a separate shower, so Dylan urged Kirsty to have a wash whilst they still had power and hot water. Dylan even managed a shave. If this was how the world was to end, the least he could do was make an effort. Lennon batted the idea of having a wash away, whilst Lucy just huffed and shrugged her shoulders. It appeared that the threat of the loss of hot water and electricity hadn't quite sunk in yet with his belligerent little daughter.

Showered and shaved, Dylan gave Lennon the task of twiddling with the radio, which brought up expected results. Nothing but static and random tunes; set into motion when dead air is broadcast for more than thirty seconds, the emergency broadcast sequence is initiated automatically. These songs would continue playing until the power to the station was finally cut off. They kept the radio on, as these three-minute songs were more than likely the last contact they would have with the outside world. It brought a strange sense of normality to proceedings.

The day reached noon and they all decided that they needed sustenance of some sort. Naturally, they used up what fresh stuff they had. It was a pessimistic thought that they should spare the tins in the cupboard for a later date.

Tomato pasta with bacon, broccoli and spinach was what Kirsty served up. They each had a coffee. Everybody cleaned their plates, though the meal sat uneasily in their stomachs as if they'd all consumed some dire, poisonous sludge.

At one o'clock, Dylan leant on the front window sill with Lennon whilst the girls cleaned up the kitchen. In the space of a few hours, more than a hundred more people had joined the mob outside.

'Getting to be quite a crowd out there,' Lennon remarked, 'wonder what they've come to see.'

For some reason, Lennon's innocent comment chilled Dylan Keene to the core of his very soul.

'Say, Dyldo, have you seen who's joined your fan club?' Lennon grinned in his typical moronic manner at a face in the crowd with a knowing nod.

'No, who?'

'Celeste.'

'Shhh . . . Celeste, Celeste?' Dylan shushed and quietened his tone so the ears in the kitchen wouldn't hear.

'Yeah, *your* Celeste.'

Dylan scanned the crowd, until he found her white form standing by the garden wall, pure alabaster, untouched by the burn of the sun which she never liked, flowing red hair down past her shoulders. She'd put a little weight on, the breasts mostly, a little round the hips, a slight jowl, but she looked good for it. Dylan always thought she'd been too thin, needed some meat on her bones.

'What's it been?' Lennon asked, quieter this time.

'Fourteen years since I've seen her.'

'I thought she moved away after you broke up?'

'So did I? Didn't think I'd see her again. Not like this anyway.'

Celeste Marks was wearing nothing but matching La Senza black lacy bra and panties, brazen and as beautiful as the day she left him, she had aged well. She would be what Lennon would describe as a Milf or even a Cougar. It appeared whatever sudden fixation with his home that struck down the crowd, had happened to Celeste in a state of undress.

'Why's she back?' Lennon asked.

'Your guess is as good as mine. I think her parents still live round here somewhere, I see her dad at the pub occasionally, never speak to him though.'

'Humph,' Lennon shrugged, 'Why would you?'

'Not a word to Kirsty, understand? She never met her.'

'Right-o,' Lennon replied with a quick salute for his brother, 'what a shame.'

Preparation is the Key

Heeding his wife's suggestion, Dylan decided that getting ready to defend his home wasn't such a bad idea. They put the idea to Lucy and Lennon who agreed. So they set to work.

Firstly, they reinforced the outer doors, screwing them shut; top, middle and bottom of the door frame using some spare screws and a Phillips. They didn't even bother with the windows, there were too many, and if they really wanted to get in, they'd get in. In the main bedroom, Dylan and Lennon shifted furniture, positioning the big wardrobe beside the door, so in the event of a forced entry from the crowd outside, they could tip the wardrobe on its side, utilising the main bedroom as a makeshift panic room. Kirsty took this one-step further by storing food and spare containers of water on the windowsill. Just in case. She even tidied up the mess of clothes that decorated the bedroom. Before, Dylan had christened this her 'floordrobe'.

Next came offence. Raiding the kitchen cupboards and drawers, they grabbed knives, brooms and mops. Detaching the broom head, Lennon securely duct taped a steak knife to the end, concocting a crude spear.

Dylan sprayed a mop head in air freshener, turning it into a makeshift torch; fire, one of mankind's greatest and devastating weapons. He hoped the dumbstruck dolts outside recognized the flaming threat.

Meanwhile, Kirsty and Lucy scoured the house for anything else that might come in handy. Batteries, torches, first aid kits. All these were stock piled in the main bedroom at the front of the house. Sensing that the stairs were a vulnerable point of entry, Kirsty and her daughter eagerly pushed a chest of drawers to the top of the stairs, ready to block off the landing. It was a meagre defence, but it might slow them down should they get inside the house. All these preparations were being carried out with a grim sense of doomed irony. If the crowd did storm the house, would they even get a chance to fight back, or would the shock of the fight strike them down as dumb as rocks.

***

'Dyl, what are we getting ready for exactly?' Lennon asked his brother as they both scoured the shelves in the adjoining garage. He moved his stickered guitar case to one side. It had been living in Dylan's garage for the past three years. Lennon leant it on top of the case containing Dylan's bass. Thankfully Harry took home his drum kit after each practice, so the garage wasn't too cramped.

'An attack,' Dylan said, grabbing a flat edged screwdriver and placing it in the red plastic tub they'd placed on the floor to collect their arsenal.

'But they haven't done anything yet.'

'But they might. Wouldn't you rather be prepared?'

'But we're getting ready to fight innocent people.'

'And?'

'What have they done to us?'

'Nothing,' Dylan responded, dropping low to rummage around the junk on the bottom shelf, then turned back to face Lennon, 'yet.'

'So why don't we just start killing them now? Y'know, set fire to them or something?' Lennon ventured.

'Because Len, that would be murder.'

'So you're telling me that we've got to wait for them to attack us before we can do anything?'

'Yep. It's called the rules of engagement. We can't fight them until they fight us. It's what makes us the moral superiority.'

'Doesn't make us smarter than them though does it?'

'What do you mean?'

'Well, they're just waiting. They're not preparing themselves, sharpening sticks and reinforcing their defences.'

'Len, they don't need to. They've got numbers. They can swarm us and give us a stomping. The best we can do is to deter them.'

'Deter them? There's like two hundred of them with more every hour. At this rate, we'll be outnumbered a hundred-to-one in no time. What's the point?' Lennon motioned to the rusty carpet knife he held in his hand, 'they won't even have to try.'

'I'm doing this for Kirsty. She's worried. Doing something constructive will make her feel better.'

Lennon swept his arm around the garage, 'all of this is just a psychological deterrent?'

'Unless you come up with a worthier way to spend our time?'

'We could fire up the Play Station?'

They both managed forced laughs, then looked at each other with mutual unease for a few seconds.

'I'm worried bro,' Lennon confessed. He toyed with the knife in his hand, sliding the rusted blade back and forth. Click. Click. Click.

'We all are,' Dylan responded.

Lennon took a step back shaking his head, 'Christ, I need a tab!'

Dylan stood up from his fruitless delving on the bottom row of junk boxes and miscellanea, 'top shelf behind you, look behind the ant powder. Don't tell Kirsty.'

Lennon shot his brother a look then investigated the hiding place. His fingers emerged with a crumpled cigarette packet. Lennon smiled as he opened the packet, revealing the remaining five.

'Dyl . . . you're a life saver.'

'Don't tell Kirsty . . .'

'Don't tell Kirsty what?' his wife interrupted from the kitchen.

Dylan shot round, Kirsty was staring at him from the kitchen table where she stood with a torch. Think . . .

'Doesn't matter darling.'

'No, what? Tell me.'

'I thought we had some petrol, so we could make some petrol bombs, y'know just in case.'

'Why would that bother me?'

'Because I told Len I was going to take the aerosol from your hairspray, make a weapon that way.'

'Why would that bother me? I'm fine with that. I've got loads of half empty bottles that I don't use because I switch brands so damned often. You're welcome to them.'

'In the bathroom cupboard?'

'Yeah.'

'I'll have a look in there next darling.'

'No worries,' Kirsty turned her back and began changing the batteries in the torch she had, 'You guys fancy a coffee?'

'Yeah.' the brothers responded in unison, both glaring relieved faces at each other. But Dylan knew that his wife finding out he was still a secret smoker would be the least of his worries today.

Lennon gave his brother a reassuring tap on the shoulder and a wink that showed his gratitude for the smokes, picked up the box of potentially dangerous wares and headed back to the kitchen, where the kettle bubbled away happily.

As he moved to leave, Dylan noticed a dull blue glint in the corner of the garage. Curiosity got the better of him and he headed over to investigate. Resting his hand on the slim painted blue handle, he pulled out the baseball bat from the dusty corner of the garage. He'd bought it years ago for Lucy, just to see if he could get her involved in sports of any kind. She'd tried trampoline lessons, dance, kickboxing, judo. None of which she took to. The baseball bat however had provided Dylan with an afternoon of joy with his daughter. They'd gone to the park and played a lazy game of rounders, he pitched while she batted and Kirsty fielded. She had managed a few good swings, knocked a few over their heads. She'd had a go and they all had a good time during a sunny day in the park. When they got back, Dylan put the bat in the corner of the garage where it had rested until now.

It had been a day of smiles, she showed no further interest in pursuing the sport any further, yet Dylan was proud and content that she'd tried. That had been about three years ago. Now she was a teenager, anything and everything was a massive, disrupting effort for her. He thought back to the last time they'd had a proper laugh together. Nothing came to mind until he remembered the day last summer when he took her for a driving lesson on the disused Brambleby airfield. He had a day off work and Lucy was off for the holidays, so as long as she didn't tell her mother about it there was nothing to worry about.

She stalled the Corsa pretty much ten times on the trot, but once she grasped the concept of the biting point they were away, even managing a larger incident free complete lap of the runway.

Afterwards she gave him a hug, probably the last time she had shown such affection towards him. He wondered if he'd ever get a chance to take her for that second drive. He'd being looking forward to it. Imparting knowledge was a gift to the elder as well as to the youth that learns.

Dylan looked out of the small window that looked out onto their back garden. Mrs Loughery was still there with a few other strangers. Still nude and staring at the house, their gazes appeared to be tilted upwards, towards the upstairs window. He watched as her head slowly tilted down back to the ground floor.

What was she looking at?

Dylan's line of sight shifted to the shed behind them at the bottom of the garden.

He had shovels and spades in there. Fuel as well, a small fire axe for chopping wood, weed killer. Hell, he had a hundred different ways of killing and incapacitating people locked up in the shed.

He looked at the bat. This will have to do for now.

Dylan picked up a rusty decking screw from an old margarine tub destined to harbour odds and ends of hardware trinkets; using a Phillips screw driver he worked the long screw into the fat end of the bat; the wood creaking as it split and made way for the addition, the cords in his arm straining as he forced metal through wood. It took him a few minutes of straining labour but he had made the slugger a little more deadly.

Christ, he thought. This has only been going on for half a day now and he was already preparing to murder strangers and neighbours. He had a right, he considered. He felt threatened in his own home. Surely that would be reasoning enough for an Englishman to have the right to defend his castle. Yeah, if somebody attacks it. So far, the only blood he had seen spilt was a guy getting run over; and that had been his own stupid fault, and the plane crash, which was more than beyond their control.

Dylan waved to Mrs Loughery, expecting to be surprised if she took notice. She stared dumbly ahead.

He took the modified bat into the kitchen, where a fresh coffee was waiting along with his brother rummaging through a box of tricks, his wife digging out a biscuit tin and his daughter, fresh from a shower and in a clean change of clothes from her nightwear. With a weary sigh, Dylan placed the bat on the kitchen table and drank his hot coffee, savouring the taste while he could.

***

As the afternoon dragged on, they had more coffee to pass the time and the crowd got larger. A few more had passed through the side gate and joined the nude Mrs Loughery in the back garden. Dylan now counted twenty strangers standing blank faced. Kirsty was always chiding him for not locking the back gate, now her warnings had come to fruition. It would have been nice to have access to the back of the house, get some sun and stretch their legs.

Lucy had come down stairs after her shower, clad in a sleeveless *SpongeBobSquarePants* t-shirt that she had customised herself, and ragged jeans, the knees scuffed away by a cheese grater, the thighs sliced open by scissors; again her own design. She'd forfeited the garish purple eye make-up she usually wore on a Saturday. Nowadays, since his daughter had approached womanhood quicker than he thought possible, he resisted the urge to comment on her dress sense, as he preferred life with as few arguments as possible whilst in the vicinity of a teenage girl under the influence of raging and turbulent hormones.

Kirsty came up to him and gave him a hug, smiled at him, and then went over and hugged her daughter, who half-heartedly returned the embrace. Lennon had headed upstairs, to smoke out the bathroom window. After the hug from his wife, Dylan went upstairs to check on his brother.

Lennon had finished his smoke, now he peered out the front bedroom window onto the expanding crowd below; grimacing at the crater the downed plane had dug out of the field. Various pieces of smoking grey shrapnel decorated the land between the house and the hole. Strange streaks of red and blackened bodies that'd been felled by the fire now lay down like scattered playing tokens of some horrific board game that played for people, not points. New strangers filled in the gaps that the dead had left, those charred and burnt becoming a carpet of corpses and assorted human shrapnel for the new arrivals to wipe their feet.

'Penny for your thoughts?'

'How about a tenner,' Lennon responded, 'or a helicopter. This is crazy. It's beyond fucked up.'

'No shit. You know how to fly one?'

'I could have a go, beats waiting for these weirdos to move on.'

Dylan grinned. 'I haven't got a helicopter.'

'I know. Be nice though, could go wherever we wanted.'

'We don't know how far this has spread.'

Lennon turned from the window and crumpled his brow. 'What a way to cast a dark cloud over things. I thought the situation was bad here, now you're suggesting this has happened all over the country, maybe even the world.'

'I'm just speculating. Who knows?' Dylan joined his brother's stance beside the window. Christ, there were a lot of them. It looked like a concert audience out there. And the Keenes were the main attraction.

'Reckon there are other people like us? Y'know trapped and not all weirded out?'

'I could almost guarantee it. The chances of us being the only ones. A billion to one. At least.'

'Is that supposed to be reassuring?'

'It's supposed to be.'

'What do we do Dyl? I know it's only been a few hours, but I'm already getting cabin fever.'

'Just try to relax and keep calm. Don't get worked up, this can't go on forever. These people have to eat at some point. We have food, enough maybe for two-three weeks with the four of us. Maybe longer, if we ration it out. They have to go home sometime. We can outlive them. There not zombies y'know.'

Lennon nodded in agreement, then leant forward and opened the window to scream, 'Why don't you lot just *fuck* off home?' Go on! Get out of here!' Lennon closed the window and smiled. None of the crowd flinched.

'What did that achieve?'

'Nothing,' Lennon grinned, 'but it made me feel better.'

The Darkening Of The Day

As the sun began to melt out a dying red into the western horizon and disappear for the day, so did their appetites. They'd eaten heartily at lunch and now as tea time approached, no one felt particularly hungry. Lucy had a bite of a banana, Kirsty nibbled an apple, while Dylan just had coffee and Lennon finished his final cigarettes straight after one another, flicking the glowing butts into the awaiting crowd below. The final one landed in the thatch like hair of a skater kid. It smoked and burned for a while, singeing out a black circle the size of a fist in the mass of hair before extinguishing itself. The kid didn't flinch as his forest of hair burned his scalp away. Lennon shuddered at his hazardous apathy and returned downstairs.

Dylan tried the radio again, getting nothing but pre-emptive pop songs playing the voices of what now seemed like ghosts. He took it as his duty to try the television again; most stations had false messages saying that normal programming would resume as soon as possible, others stated that they were experiencing technical difficulties. A few simply had shots of empty news desks or skewed angles of desolate television studios. Dylan turned off the television and turned to his family who all sat on the sofa, hoping for a semblance of sentient life outside the four closing walls.

'I think we should sleep in shifts tonight. Just to keep an eye on our friends outside, I don't want to be taken by surprise.'

Lennon narrowed his eyes and nodded at his brother's suggestion, as did Kirsty. Lucy did nothing except remain slumped on the sofa with her arms crossed, doing that terrific impression of a moody teenager she accomplished so well.

'I'll take first shift, then Len, then Kirsty and Lucy to see us through until morning. Everybody okay with that?'

Again, a nod, a nod, a sullen face.

'You okay Luce?' Dylan asked, 'you okay with that?'

'I want to see my friends,' Lucy said as blunt as a rock.

'You can't darling, the people outside might hurt us.'

'They haven't tried to hurt us. Not yet anyway,' Lucy reasoned.

'Your father's right honey, there's no telling what they'd do. I don't trust them. Even if some of them we think of as friends and neighbours are out there.'

Dylan looked outside. Mr Singha, the Spar shop owner, stood in the crowd, his dark skin slack with passive seriousness. Next, he recognized Mrs Williams, the kindly old lady from three doors down who used to babysit Lucy; Gary from work; Kirsty's friend Lisa; Lennon's druggy mate Bazza; all locals amongst a sea of strangers. A young familiar face stood out; Lucy's best friend Poppy.

'Luce, if you really want to see your friends, Poppy's outside.'

'What?' Lucy said, rising up from the sofa.

'It's Poppy, look she's one of them now. I'm sorry,' he said flat and morose; apologising for something that wasn't even his fault.

'No.'

'Yes, I'm sorry.'

Lucy stepped up to the window and pressed her palms against the glass. Maybe forty people were crowded onto the front lawn alone; you could see all their faces as their garden sloped down from the road towards the house. Immediately, she picked out the face of Poppy Smith, catatonic, wearing nothing more than a dressing gown tied loosely at the waist. Her eyes glared into the house towards Lucy, who began to cry.

'No!' Lucy banged hard on the window, the pane rumbled with a cushioned echo, she banged harder and harder, slapping her palms on the sun warmed glass. Kirsty and Lennon got up from the sofa and approached.

'Poppy! No, not you, not you . . .'

Lucy's voice deteriorated into shrieking sobs as she slumped to her knees. Dylan bent low to comfort her, but she threw off his embrace with a jarring elbow. She clambered back to her feet and stormed upstairs, each footfall echoing through the house, threatening to rattle nails from their fixings.

'Well,' Dylan shrugged, 'what was I supposed to say to her? She wanted to see her friends. I can't win.'

'It's not about winning with teenage girls, Dyly, it's about finding middle ground,' Kirsty interjected.

'Middle ground? Her best friend has turned into a brainless zombie and is now standing outside on our lawn. How am I supposed to find middle ground with them fuckers out there? Tell me! She just flies off the handle like a mentalist, you can't reason with her.'

'She's just upset, she's just reacting to this a bit strongly. She might think she's grown up, but she's still a child at the same time.'

'I don't need this Kirst. Not now. I need calm. I need everybody to be calm and collected and just listen to me. I don't want us to die . . .'

'Guys?' Lennon said quietly.

'We'll be okay; we just have to stay inside.'

'I plan to do exactly that, if she wants to go outside and talk make-up and boys with Poppy that's fine with me, but she's got to start listening and not exploding at every opportunity...'

'Say guys, look,' Lennon continued. This time he pointed.

'Just bear with her,' Kirsty defended, 'please...'

'For Christ sake, can you two look outside?'

'What?' Dylan half shouted, turning to follow the direction of Lennon's pointing finger. Kirsty did likewise.

Outside, in the garden, on the path and on the road, everybody in the crowd had their heads bent up towards the upstairs of the house. Everybody.

'Lucy will you come downstairs please... it's important,' Kirsty beckoned.

Lucy screamed something back that was too high pitched for Dylan's adult ears to comprehend.

'Lucy! Get down here now!' her father barked

A second of pause followed by the exasperated tone of a curse word, then came the thunderous stomps down the stairs. Dylan, Kirsty and Lennon watched as the crowd's gaze returned in unison to ground floor level.

Lucy barged back into the living room, face of thunder, tone of petulance. 'What?' she said, her voice curt and angry.

'Stay here.' Dylan then beckoned his wife and brother upstairs. Dutiful and curious, they followed.

'Why?' Lucy snapped in a *duh* tone.

'Just stay there sweetie,' Kirsty cooed, 'this won't take a second.'

Lucy swore again as her family headed upstairs without her.

Dylan moved onto the landing window and looked down on the crowd below; all eyes were set on downstairs.

'They didn't follow us.'

Lennon nodded, as did Kirsty.

'Luce come upstairs will you darling?'

'For christsake dad, will you please make your mind up, you're driving me mad!' Lucy stomped back up the stairs; her fuming face surged towards them on the end of the landing, 'what now!'

'Look outside.'

'At what?'

'They're all staring at you.'

Lucy stepped forward, inching her way between her mother and uncle. She stopped by her father and looked down on the mass of faces below. They were all staring up at her.

'Lucy, these people are here for you, want to tell me why?' Dylan asked, looking down at his daughter, her gaze just as perplexed as he felt.

'I don't know, I . . .' her voice trailed off and her bottom lip began to quiver. Tears pooled in her reddened eyes. Dylan wanted answers, his daughter knew something. Everybody outside was looking directly at her. Their eyes followed her around like dutiful puppies on a biscuit.

'Tell them about the dream,' Lennon put forward, hoarse and quiet, the tone wasn't his to use. He was being serious for once.

So she did. She told them everything.

***

Her mother's false smile. A close up, she remembered. A series of images, like a movie trailer, a greater amount of time but condensed.

The car crash; she even knew the colour of the poor guy's hat. That starts the dream, *a crowd of faces,* some strange, some familiar, gather round, until she can't count anymore.

Pans, cups, buckets all brimming with water. Just images, no correlation or standing in the dream.

She had described what had happened so far, all of which he could agree on. As for the cold beans, Dylan guessed at some point they'd be eating beans from a tin. Maybe the power would go out.

People digging, she had said, *fingernails breaking against rocks in the hard, compacted soil.*

He was stumped with that one; the same went for her vision of the man in the coat made of skin, and the fire close but not too far away. Maybe the plane that crashed earlier. Now the summer winds carried the raging heat towards them. Another thing to worry about.

An ache in her stomach, maybe she'd get food poisoning at some point, he thought grimly.

'Have you had dreams like this before?' Dylan asked.

'Not like this one,' Lucy replied, 'not this real.'

'Is this dream anything to do with the boy from school?' Dylan asked.

'Why would you even ask that? He wasn't in the dream. It's not about him,' Lucy shot back with a snap of her tongue.

'Lucy!' Kirsty defended, 'as strange as it may sound, your father thinks that your dream might be connected to what's going on outside.'

'I have to ask. Who's the man in the dream? Do you know him?'

'Never met him, he's a stranger. But he seemed to know me.'

'How do you mean?'

'The way he looks at me. It's funny.'

'Funny, how?'

'Just a crazy look, hungry, I don't know, just weird.'

'What's he doing in the dream, tell me exactly.'

'I'm in the living room downstairs,' Lucy looked down at her feet and sighed, 'I'm ... err, I'm naked ... I think.'

'It's okay sweetie, we all have strange dreams. Carry on.'

'Okay, I look out the front window and this man, he's good looking, like a movie star, he could be famous, he just has that look, well he walks up the driveway in this strange coat, right up to the window and looks in, straight at me and smiles.'

'Does he speak, say anything?'

'No, but there's one thing I haven't told you, that I didn't want to tell you...'

'What? Why?' Kirsty queried.

'In the dream, the carpet is soaking. I look down. You, Dad and Uncle Lenny. You're all dead. I think I killed you...'

The Heat of the Long Night

'That's not gonna happen darling.' Dylan put his hand on his daughter's shoulder, giving it a reassuring squeeze.

'I know I'd never want to hurt you guys. You're my parents, I know that I can be a bit of a bitch sometimes, but I do love you, you know that don't you?' Lucy looked at them both as earnest and as loving as she could, dimpling her cheeks to pleading sweetness.

'Of course sweet pea,' Dylan answered, squeezing her shoulder harder.

'It's just that if it does come true, you will try and stop me, won't you?'

'It's not going to happen Lucy.' Kirsty gave a half laugh, before moving in for a supporting hug, again Dylan squeezed her shoulder. Despite her dreams, they'd stick by her. They were her parents after all. Some stupid dream wasn't going to change that.

'But if I do. If I try . . . Please stop me. Don't let me do it!' Lucy's voice moved higher, she shook her head as if to rattle free the notion of parenticide from her troubled young mind.

'You won't darling; it was just a stupid little dream. It doesn't mean anything,' Kirsty reasoned.

'But it does. Everything else has come true so far. I hate it!' Lucy buried her face into her mother's chest, the anguish flowed freely now.

'It was just a dream, don't worry too much about it.' Dylan shot his wife a concerned, though reassuring look, shaking his head, '. . . shhhhush, just a dream.'

'Just promise me . . . if I do go crazy, knock me out, tie me up, just don't let me hurt any of you!'

'It won't come to that . . .' Dylan reckoned.

'Promise!'

'I promise. Just tell us when, give us notice if possible okay? If you're gonna go schizoid on us, give us a heads up at least kiddo.'

'I'll do my best, Dad.' Lucy turned, and fell into her father, embracing him as tight as her arms would allow.

Outside, as darkness had fallen as it should; one by one, the street lights flickered on, right on time, illuminating the mass of bodies with an orange glow from another world.

***

Sitting around the kitchen table with Lucy drinking apple juice, they tried to stomach their coffees. Sinking them down through a false veneer of vague smiles, they laughed as Lennon told a few dirty jokes to lighten the mood. Even as the laughter carried on further into the evening, Dylan couldn't help but feel foreboding fingers creeping up the rungs of his spine. Their laughter was real, he was sure of that. But was it that they were just getting in one last laugh before the world crumbled around them all. There was no nervousness, no anticipation on show. Lucy was getting on with Lennon, his family was being genuine for once, and this was how they felt. Infected with laughter, it was good. It was true.

Happy to be alive.

They could be splattered on the pavement, they could be trapped inside the burning wreckage of an airliner doomed by gravity after the pilot, crew and passengers were hypnotised by mind rays from Mars.

They could be outside.

The laughter was just their thankful human nature coming out. Maybe it was down to nervousness, and all this was just an act. The scene outside the front (and back) door played into his mind after he laughed at the punch line of another of Lennon's filthy jokes.

They were doomed to die, in one way or another. It could be tomorrow, could be in a hundred years' time. It didn't matter. But the strange threat outside intensified the stifling feeling he felt creeping round his neck like an invisible garrotte. This was the final laugh. There has to be a final everything, right? The last kiss, that final drive to work before you smash into a bus driven without enough due care and attention, the remnants of the meal that will remain inside you when they lower you into the ground and cover you in six feet of fine, cold soil. The last dance, the last time you squint wearily at the morning sun. It all adds to the same equation. You don't know when you're going to go, so make it count. That's why their laughter was so infectious. Just in case, it's the last time. At one point, the laughter became too much, Lucy didn't even get the joke but she was laughing with sheer joy at her parents' reactions, especially her mother's shock and a few choice dirty words that had spouted from her uncle's mouth. They'd become hysterical as the madness of the situation was drowned out by their commune of humanity. But soon, the humour abated, and they all calmed down to a reasonable level.

'Mind if I have a beer, Dyldo?' Lennon asked, getting up and heading towards the fridge.

'Just one bro, I'd rather make them last.'

'Sure no worries, I'll take it steady,' Lennon said as he opened the fridge door, reached in, grabbed a Bud, placed it in his mouth and dented it with his incisors, then popped it open by trapping it with his molars.

'I wish you wouldn't do that,' Kirsty protested, 'you'll ruin your teeth.'

'I'll be fine. My teeth will stay where they are until they're punched out.' Lennon smiled, dropping the bottle cap in the bin. He returned to the table, choosing to remain standing. 'Is it getting hot in here, or is it just me?'

'It is a bit.' Kirsty responded, blowing air up across her face as if to illustrate the fact. She fanned herself, but it did little good.

'It's them outside, it's their body heat.'

Lennon's eyes widened, his brow crinkling 'Really? Y'reckon?'

'Can't be anything else, wasn't too warm today. Now there are lots of them, their combined heat is essentially going to cook us from the inside out.'

'Not literally though, don't exaggerate darling,' Kirsty corrected.

'I hope not, but the way today has gone it wouldn't surprise me.'

Everybody smiled wryly, Lennon chugged back some beer.

'Can't we open a window or something? Change the air?' Lucy suggested.

'Hell no! I don't want to give them a way in,' Lennon protested.

'They'll just stand there won't they?' said Lucy, 'if they wanted to get in, I think that they would have already.'

'That may be . . .' Dylan thought for a second, then, 'okay, upstairs windows only, and keep them on the latches.'

'Cheers, Dad!' Lucy glowed, whilst getting up from the table, 'I think I'll go to bed now if that's okay? If Mum and I are doing the last shift, I'd like to be fresh.'

'I reckon that might be a good idea, are you going to bed darling?' Dylan casually asked his wife, as if the hordes outside didn't exist at all, as if this were a normal prelude to slumber.

'Yeah I think so. Why not?' she said as she leant over and kissed Dylan tenderly on the forehead. 'Don't worry, I won't open the window too far.'

'I know you won't.'

'Good night Papa Bear.' Lucy too kissed her father, this time on the cheek. He couldn't remember the last she had kissed him so sweetly. He had thought that he was losing her to the weird, wide world, new friends and that word he dreaded; *boys*. Evidently, he was still her Papa Bear, a nickname she had endearingly called him from the ages of three to eleven. Nostalgia swelled his heart.

'Good night, sweetheart.'

'Good night girls,' added Lennon with a gormless grin, waving his hand in an over enthusiastic *bon voyage*. He sat down, took another chug of beer. The rim popped as he pulled it away from lips, and then placed the half empty bottle on the table.

The girls headed upstairs to bed. They heard windows opening and sighs of relief as the humid atmosphere of the house was lost and exchanged to the outside. Lennon turned and leaned into his brother and said, 'right; what the fuck are we going to do?'

'About what?'

'*Them.*'

'The Starers?'

'Don't give them a name,' Lennon scolded.

'*Them* is a name.'

'Doesn't sound as ominous as *The Starers*.' Lennon stood up and removed his t-shirt, revealing his mild case of beer belly beneath. He wiped the sweat from his chest and head, then dropped the t-shirt over the back of the chair.

'Sounds like a horror movie,' Lennon moved his hands up beside his head and tickled the air with tingling clawed fingers, then in an ominous gravelly voice he announced, '*The Starers! Coming soon . . ., or are they already here? Watching you take a shit!*'

Dylan laughed; Lennon sat back down, the sweat of his back sliding him down into the leather chair with a damp squeak.

'Christ it's hot! I feel like I could peel my skin off and hang it up,' declared Lennon, 'so what'll we do?'

'I say we wait.'

'You on about them outside; *The Starers?*'

'Of course.'

'Do you not fancy a break to the car; see how far we can get?'

'Not particularly, no. In case one of them bastards out there suddenly turns hungry and bites my head off.'

'I'll go.'

'I'm not losing you Lennon. We've already lost Mum and Dad in this past year. No. End of.'

'Just a thought; an experiment at most.'

'No. Don't even risk it.'

'Can I have another beer then?' Lennon looked down on Dylan with oh-so-earnest cute puppy dog eyes. He even fluttered his eyelashes like a flirting whore.

'Last one. But pour me half.'

'Deal.' Lennon downed his Bud and headed back to the fridge to obtain another, opening it in the traditional teeth cracking manner. He grabbed a glass from off the counter top, pouring Dylan just less than half. He didn't mind. He wasn't really in the mood for booze. He was just being social.

The Keene brothers talked as the night boiled on. They talked about girls that they'd gone to school with and the one in particular that Lennon had made moves on last week, getting nowhere but a cop of a tit and a midnight fumble. Dylan talked about work, telling some of his work mates jokes, places he'd been and funny stories of the road. When he suggested that Lennon try for a job with the company, he shot it down as soon as the sentence had left Dylan's mouth.

'You'd get sick of working with me; you'd hate me after eight hours on the road.'

'You wouldn't necessarily be with me; you'd be another driver's mate most of the time. It'll be easy money.'

'I'll think about it.'

'Monday morning, I want you dropping off a CV, no excuses.'

Lennon paused, thought for a moment then nodded in the direction of the front room. 'You're talking like there's an end to all this.'

'Everything has to end at some point, they can't stand out there forever, they need food and sleep, and they're still human y'know.'

'How so we know that, they might have been brainwashed by Martians for all we know.'

'That's doubtful.'

'How do you think it'll end? All this fucked-up-ness.' Lennon gestured all around with a sweep of his hand.

'Well, looking at it straight and being totally honest, it can either go two ways. If they don't move they'll starve of malnutrition and drop down dead one by one. But if they don't succumb to starvation and outlast us, we'll die first. But before that happens, I'd happily go out there with a burning torch and start to set alight to the bastards.'

'You'd do that?' Lennon asked.

'If it meant my family surviving I would. But only as a last resort. When we're on the last tin of beans.'

Lennon smiled to himself, 'the last tin of beans scenario. I like it.'

'Well I don't.' Dylan yawned, stretched his arms, letting his elbows pop with gratitude, releasing pent up energy gathered from the strain of the day.

'If you wanna finish your shift early, you can. I'll keep an eye on things down here,' Lennon offered.

'You sure?'

'Yeah, I'll flick through the television channels; see if I can find anything. I'll holler if anything kicks off.'

'Cheers man, I'm beat. Just let me get a few hours in and I'll be back down.'

'Get some shuteye, you've had one hell of a bad day.'

'Thanks bro. We all have. Okay, g'night'

Dylan drained the dregs from his Bud then pushed himself wearily up from the table. His legs wobbled from sitting down for so long. He smiled once at Lennon, and then headed upstairs to bed.

Kirsty was sharing the bed with Lucy, his place taken up by his daughter's slight frame. He considered sliding into bed with them, but they looked so peaceful he had no immediate desire to wake them. He'd let them be. He'd already spent a night on the sofa and wasn't that entirely keen on repeating that cramped position. He needed a bed tonight, he deserved it. He'd take Lucy's bed.

First, seeing as they still had water, Dylan washed his face and brushed his teeth. He grabbed a glass and filled it, drinking a pint of water just to hydrate his body while he could.

The floorboards creaked in protest as he made his way into Lucy's room. She hadn't made the bed, but he was too tired to care. Dylan opened a window, his eyes catching the gaze of the forty or so random people that congregated in the rear garden, their blank eyes reflecting the bright light of the high moon. He watched for a second as two more strangers filed in through the back gate and took up position by the shed. He didn't recognize them, they were unknowns to him.

He stripped down to his boxer shorts before slipping beneath the cool covers that instantly began absorbing the heat from his body and reflecting it back. He kicked the covers off to expose as much of himself to the sticky night air as possible. He lay for a while, thinking how strange it was not to hear the susurration of passing car tyres on the road outside. Usually at this time on a Saturday night, taxis would be ferrying drunken revellers back from town. He heard nothing but the deafening hum of tearing silence in his own ears. He couldn't hear what Lennon was up to downstairs. The utter quiet was unnerving. Soon his breathing slowed enough as tiredness took over and Dylan Keene began to melt away into deep and welcome slumber.

An Unfamiliar House

Dylan stands in the middle of the road; he is barefoot, wearing only jeans and a white t-shirt. He doesn't own a crisp white t-shirt this clean, he muses. He can't see the white lines that divide the road in two as discarded clothes surround him, male and female, adult and child, each arranged in crumpled piles. Strangely, socks are stuffed into shoes; shirts still have ties on round collars. Watches, handbags and spectacles litter the field of garments. He thinks rapture, and assumes that he's been left behind to clear up the mess.

In his ears, he can hear the pop and crackle of what sounds like Rice Krispies snapping up moisture as they drown in milk. It's a familiar noise that he's heard somewhere else.

Before him stands his home, his neighbours' properties seem plain and uninteresting compared to his house, grey almost. He ignores them and concentrates on his. Some windows are broken, guttering hangs off; the front lawn is chewed up from wear and tear. Their car is missing. Again, clothes litter the driveway and what's left of the lawn.

A voice calls that makes no noise, but he feels the impotent sound wave stroke his eardrums, causing him to turn. His looks north, up the road towards the Catchwater junction about a hundred metres away. *The Green Tree* sits on the corner, the pub car park empty of cars, but chock full of clothes.

Across from the pub, stood in the middle of the road parallel to Dylan, stands a figure, stark against the parade of empty garments. The figure looks like Kirsty, she's stood there, wearing similar attire to him. She stands still and stares at him with grey eyes. Not moving. He offers a hand and waves, she remains stoic and Golem like.

Dylan moves towards her, she turns and starts to walk away from him. He breaks into a jog, strangers clothes grab at his ankles like tentacles, congesting his path and clogging his run. He looks up, Kirsty is further away. A pair of jeans bunches up around his ankles, he trips and falls into the jumbled carpet of clothes. His head lands next to a set of yellowing false teeth; he can make out smears of food caught between the lone, grinning gnashers.

Dylan gets up, pushing himself up of off the garmented lawn; Kirsty is gone. Vanished. He spots a white t-shirt floating to the ground up ahead, melding into the colourful tapestry of denim, cotton and polyester that now make up the hidden surface of Westfield Road.

Another sense of sound vibrates mutely against his eardrum, a voice calling. He looks down Westfield Road, where the lay of the land dips as it nears the edge of town. Lucy stands there in the middle of the road. White t-shirt, blue denims.

He gets up to chase her, but like her mother, she too turns and runs in the opposite direction. Dylan makes more of an effort this time. Leaping over the piles of clothes, he will catch up to her.

The faster he runs, the quicker he'll make a mistake and soon his bare foot snags a shoe and he tumbles, but he keeps his balance and bounds on. In front of him, Lucy's glossy obsidian hair flaps and bounces like the wings of an escaping bird. Dylan draws nearer; he's going to catch her. He cries out her name, but no sound voices from his neutered throat. He stretches his fingers; index finger and thumb come into contact with the fine filament of Lucy's silken black hair. Then without any clue or commotion, Lucy vanishes, her clothes continue for a few more steps without her then cascade to the ground as if she were part of a conjurer's illusion. Dylan runs into them, grabs them and holds onto them, a prayer wishing that she would suddenly inflate back into her clothes. She doesn't. He cries out, a still, mute scream forced up against an unfamiliar sky, stilted and swirling like a grey whirlpool, momentum gaining, soon it will become a vortex.

Another voice, calm and collected, hums a sweet old tune. He senses that it comes from inside his house. Now alone and with a definite concern about the turbulent sky, Dylan gets up, reluctant, he leaves Lucy's empty clothes to be lost amongst the rest of them. He treads steadily, careful not to trip again as he moves down the drive. A glint despite the grey light. His car keys rest on someone's shoe. Keys but no car. He must have parked it somewhere else, he shrugs.

Some of the smashed windows are bust outwards, some lean inwards. Whatever happened here happened inside and outside the house at the same time, he reasons.

The lock is broken on the front door; the handle hangs limply, pointing downwards like an impotent appendage. With a push, the door swings inwards, inviting Dylan in like a hungry open mouth.

The gloom swallows him as he steps inside. Behind him he feels the sky darken, the light fades from grey to black, rushing forward like a black wall. Dylan closes the door behind him, knowing that he can do nothing to secure it now. If something wants to get in, it'll get in. He ventures further into his home, except this can't be his house, as it's impossibly black, like striding into a wall of black oil.

'Evening bro,' a disembodied voice calls as he enters the living room. Dylan feels the cool blackness chill his skin.

Dylan mouths a response but no sound emits from his lips.

'I understand,' the voice seems to smile, 'sit down, it's your house after all.'

Where? Dylan thinks.

A light erupts from the nothingness, Lennon's smile appears over a Zippo flame, it's his smile but the face isn't his. It's mostly skull with the occasional patch of dark sticky flesh attached to the smooth bone of the skull. He still has eyes, which stare at Dylan from above the single eye of a dancing flame, sitting in the roomy sockets of his face. His eyes are lidless pools.

Christ what happened?

'Got in a fight, but I'm okay. A few scratches. Nothing more.'

A few scratches? It looks like someone's kicked your face off! Who did this?

'Who do you think? It was a little fight, I'll be fine. It'll heal.'

Dylan looked down at Lennon's clothes; they too were stained with blood. Thick, black blood cloaked him like tar. When he talked, Dylan could see the bruised tendons that held his jaw together stretch and retract with each forming word. He could even imagine what the smell was like; not yet rotting, but an unpleasant fustiness that offended the nostrils. A human knowing that death was in the air. You don't know it until you smell it. And when you do, it chills you to your core.

Hope you got a few punches in.

'I'd like to say that, but there were too many of them. You know that.'

Dylan nodded.

What do you want?

'I want you to be safe, bro. I want you and your girls to get through this alive. That's all that matters now, understand?'

Did you think that I didn't want that?

'Ha, god no. But you've got to get out of the house, you've got to escape, get as far away from here as you can.'

Why, what do you know that I don't?

'I don't know much, but I know one thing, you've got to get away from this place, just run, move as far away from here as you can as fast as you can. You think I'm joking when I say get a helicopter.'

How? There's too many of them.

'You'll find a way. Fight through them, it won't be easy but you've got to try.'

Why what's happening?

Lennon looked at his blood soaked shoes for a second. Dylan followed his gaze. The floor was soaked with black blood as well, maybe a good inch thick, now soaked into a ruined carpet. It didn't smell fresh. It smelt like autumnal dead leaves and a copper penny on the tongue. Kirsty would go mental.

The television flickered on, the screen was cracked, but Dylan could still make out Celeste Marks dancing in an abandoned warehouse, she wasn't wearing the bra and panties. She wasn't wearing anything, yet somehow her nudity, her nipples, the fire tinged redness of her crotch seemed to remain blurred and out of focus. Like he hadn't paid enough to view everything, he wasn't privy to the full subscription just yet.

You can't have her and you can't have this! A strange voice screamed at him inside his head.

'He's coming. And when he gets here, he's going to hurt anybody who stands in his way. And I mean really hurt. He wants you to beg for death. He likes it.'

Who?

'I can't say, just don't be here when he arrives. They've already started. It won't be long, there's a lot of them, so a day or two, maybe less, and he'll be here.'

Who?

'I think we both know who I'm talking about. . .'

And with that, a brilliant white light exploded into the dream, the skinless Lennon's last grim smile was lost with the darkness. Dylan tripped through the darkness, stumbled over himself and fell awake with a breath clawed from dead, tasteless air.

'Dylan? Dylan?'

A New Dawn, a New Day

'Dylan? Dylan?'

The earth moved, he was in an unfamiliar bed, which briefly unnerved him as he came too. A voice, familiar and tinged with concern, seemed to be the centre of the movement. He was moist with sweat, the bedclothes tangled around his limbs in fusty, damp twists.

'Dylan wakeup darling,' the voice said with feigned sweetness, 'how many beers did you have last night?'

Groggily and weary, he sat up. His throat had closed somewhat and his eyes felt dry and used up. He felt tired, as if the sleep had done nothing to aid his rest. If anything, he felt worse. It wasn't as dark as when he went to sleep, but the grey light of dawn had started to seep through the fabric cracks in the curtains.

'Whatsamata?' Dylan croaked, twisting the ball of his hand into his eye socket.

'You best come down stairs. It's Lennon.'

The dream came flooding back in a startling wave. Imagining flurries of blood, Dylan shot bolt upright in bed. Alertness washed through him and he opened his eyes. He had slept in Lucy's bedroom. When he realised why, the whole horrible nightmare came rushing back to him. Kirsty stood over him, her expression tight and grey with concern. His eyes ticked left and right, taking in the room, asserting any immediate danger. He discovered none, just the calm and peace of the tranquil morning, yet he detected a hint of smoke and sulphur in the air. Then he remembered the plane and a shudder ran through him.

Had all those people really died?

'What?' he asked, blinking away the tired ghost of sleep that still haunted him.

'It's your brother.'

'What's up with him?'

'You'd best see for yourself.' Kirsty warned, her expression softened a little bit.

Dylan jumped out of bed, grabbed his jeans and pulled them on. Still buttoning his fly, he rushed downstairs, nearly tripping in the process.

Lennon was on the living room floor. Lucy stood over him, arms crossed with a face like thunder, a deep scowl that made her look older and more like her mother on a bad day. Beer bottles littered the floor, about eight in total, as well as an empty Jack Daniels bottle and half a bottle of Navy rum. The cap was missing and a portion of the sweet stickiness had flowed from out of the bottle and onto the living room carpet, creating a brown stain that sort of resembled a disfigured and bent Jesus. Dylan bent down and got closer to Lennon's face, which rested in a drying puddle of his own dark yellow vomit. This phlegm infused rejection of beer and bile looked less like Jesus and more like a Jackson Pollock creation.

'Len?' Dylan spoke with croaking weariness. He nudged his brother once on the shoulder, then a little harder when he didn't respond. Kirsty joined her daughter in a judgemental pose. Arms crossed, face taut, mainlining that severe beauty that they both exuded.

'Lennon?' He gave him another shove, harder this time.

Lennon groaned. His face moved a little, pulling the vomit away from the carpet like melted cheddar stuck to his cheek. He groaned again, moved a hand up to his forehead and slapped it gently.

'UH?' a single grunted syllable, a poor attempt at a word.

'What happened bro? You've finished the beers and my birthday whisky. Why?'

'Uhh . . . no.'

'What, no what?' Dylan asked.

'No . . . more . . . beer. Not for me . . . urrr, thank you.'

'No, I'm not asking if you want another beer. I'm asking why you drank the rest of the beer, the rum and spewed it up all over the carpet?'

'I'm in trouble, yeah?' he growled

'Even I'm pissed at you Len. Now get up you fucking dolt!' Dylan's tone became sharper, a little more unforgiving.

'Can't.'

'Get up Len!' Dylan only called Lennon Len when he meant business. But because he loved his brother, this was a rare occasion.

'No . . .'

Dylan slipped his arms underneath Lennon's and hoisted him up to his feet. A groan of protest was followed by Lennon becoming rigid. He then spun round and swung out. A slack fist caught Dylan in the mouth, vomit stained knuckles scratched flesh away as two fingers poked slickly over his tongue, chafing against his incisors.

'Gerrrofff!'

Lennon punched again with his other arm, a little more power this time, catching him under the jaw, bruising his throat. Dylan gagged, not just from the invading fingers but from the rancid, bitter smell they gave off. He reared up and fell, a foot slipped over a beer bottle that rolled smoothly and efficiently beneath the arch of his foot. He tried to turn but fell back hard against the flat expanse of the tiled fireplace. His brain rattled and thumped around the confines of his skull. A blinding burst of pain exploded through the grey light of the approaching dawn as Dylan recounted and struggled to come to terms with what had just happened. He played the situation over and over again, wondering when he could have got a parting shot in at his brother. The grey light spun away like dirty bathwater down a plughole. Then barely three minutes after waking up, Dylan was forced back to sleep as his brief consciousness ebbed away, stolen from his shore like a secluded moonlit tide.

***

Light had fully arrived when Dylan came to. He felt wet on the side of his head. A jarring coolness dribbled down the back of his head, causing him to shiver, which brought him round further. He tried to get up. A soft hand forced him back down.

'Stay,' she whispered. 'You've bumped your head.'

'Len?' he questioned.

'He's sorry,' Kirsty said. 'He's ashamed of what he did. He said he didn't mean it.'

Dylan opened his eyes to see that the curtains were open, fresh light spilled into the living room. He was laid on the sofa; Kirsty was knelt before him, pressing a cold flannel to the left side of his head. He squinted, and then closed his eyes again.

'Len?' he asked again.

'He went upstairs. Don't fight. We don't need it.'

Dylan pushed himself off the sofa, Lucy entered from the kitchen with a glass of water.

'I thought you'd like a drink.'

Dylan smiled at his daughter's kindness and took the glass, taking a sip. His throat glistened with thanks at the brief dreg.

'Just try and rest please Dylan. I don't want a fuss.'

'He punched me. I need to know why. I can't let that rest.'

Kirsty said nothing; she pulled away, removing the cold compression from the side of his head. The throbbing pain started to flow back as hot blood flooded into the bruise.

'I'm off to see him. This needs sorting.'

Again, Kirsty said nothing. Dylan took another sip of water and handed the glass back to Lucy. As he moved back to the door, he noticed the gathered crowd outside the front window shoulder to shoulder. There were more of them. A lot more. A sea of blank, unknowing faces stared stoically back at him. Well, Lucy to be precise.

Lennon was on the landing, he had a lit cigarette in his fingers, the window was wide open and he was blowing smoke outside. In his hand, he played with his Zippo, the one from the dream, turning it over and over in his fingers. Although it was just an innocent object, somehow it seemed like an ominous memento.

'Hey bro, how's the hangover?' Dylan asked.

'Never mind that, how's your head?' he said, his expression solemn and scorned.

'I'll live.'

'I am sorry, I was tetchy and drunk. I apologise.' Lennon looked at him as earnest as he could muster, 'I'm really sorry.'

'I know you didn't mean to Len. I just want to know why?'

'I don't know. Fear? I had a dream last night that those *things* were after me. Chasing me down street after street, I'd get more and more tired, and they'd get closer, but never catch up with me. It was horrible. I couldn't wake up, I couldn't get away. I just had to keep running.'

Dylan's dream tore through his mind's eye like a locomotive. He wanted to tell Lennon about what he saw, but something held him back. He didn't have the heart to confess to him that he'd met with an undead version of his brother whilst bound by slumber.

'Did you dream Dyl?' Lennon asked, taking another toke on his cigarette.

'I slept like a baby until Kirsty woke me up. So I must have needed it.' He gave a slight cough of a laugh, not even convincing himself.

Lennon raised one eyebrow suspiciously, as if he already knew there was more to the matter. But thankfully for Dylan, he didn't push it.

'I thought you'd had your last smoke?'

'I had half, and then stubbed it out. I was trying to ration. You want the last bit?'

'Sure,' Dylan approached the landing window without fear and took the last smoke in the entire house from his brother. He borrowed Lennon's lighter and lit it. About an inch was left; it felt like he was taking the contraband off a man waiting to face the firing squad.

Dylan put it to his lips and inhaled, exhaling the sweet smoke above the heads of the crowd. He handed the lighter back to Lennon, then Dylan looked out the window; the crater from the plane was still smouldering; vagaries of smoke fingered sporadically towards the charcoal sky, though he couldn't see any lit fires. The worst must have been over. The side of the house closest to the field was polluted with soot from the fire; it spread around the front of the house with static, black, billowing fingers that held onto the house with a deathly grasp.

'A lot more of them this morning, you can hardly see the ground for faces,' Lennon noted. He tapped the Zippo on the windowsill, rotating it over and over with his thumb and index finger. He was agitated by the situation.

'Yup,' Dylan responded, then, 'why'd you drink all that booze?'

Lennon sighed then blew air from between his lips, 'Dunno, stress maybe, fear, stupidity?' He paused and pulled that puppy dogface. 'Sorry about the carpet.'

'Say that to Kirsty, she picked it out.'

'The vomit?'

'The carpet.'

Lennon smiled sheepishly, 'I'll clean it up. I'll scrub it new.'

With a sweet remembrance of when he smoked full time, Dylan tugged his breath through the self destructive cigarette then flicked the ember into the waiting crowd below.

'I know you will.'

Lennon smiled. Dylan did not. He looked down at Celeste Marks, who in turn looked at his daughter through the front window. Celeste Marks, the girl of his dreams, right there waiting for him, teasing him. Celeste Marks, the girl who turned down his marriage proposal, who shredded his heart, pissed him off so much he punched his own boss in a drunken rage, losing his once promising job as a recording studio's new apprentice assistant. If things were different, he'd be married to her and would have been a top music producer by now no doubt. That had been the dream. The fantasy of the future had been a lie. He'd been told that he had an ear for talent. Music had been destiny, delivering computer parts had been his fate.

Celeste Marks; taunting him from his past made him shiver.

'Just to get things straight,' said Dylan coolly, 'if you'd pulled what you did this morning, on any other day,' he pointed outside to the crowd, 'and if they weren't outside and we weren't trapped in here. I wouldn't have hesitated to put your lights out right about now. You're my brother and I love you. But you're lucky to still have your jaw intact, any other day and things would be very different right now . . .'

'Dyl, listen . . .' Lennon tried.

'No, *you* listen,' he placed his hand firmly on his brothers shoulder, and squeezed hard, digging his fingers in, 'I'm trying to keep this family together despite the circumstances. I feel like a right bastard for the effort as well. My wife probably hates me for what I said to Lucy. Lucy hates me, because . . . she just does, and you . . . you're a fucking idiot for that stunt you pulled last night. I wouldn't be surprised if we all ended up killing each other. . .'

'Don't say that Dyl. I'm sorry all right, I wasn't thinking straight. It's them outside, they've got me worried, wound up like. Y'know, like it would be the last time I got drunk.'

'You were drunk the night before!'

'You know me, I'm weak-willed. I can't say no. The beer was just sitting there. I couldn't *not* drink it.'

'Yes you could. It's called willpower, and respect. Here's me rationing food and water and there's you supping every last bit of booze in the house like a crazed pig.'

'I only drank half the rum, and I think you'll find I left you a beer in the fridge,' Lennon protested, half proud.

'Well gee, thanks Len. That's much appreciated. What about the JD?'

'Don't be like that Dyl . . .'

'You made me like this Len! For all I know I've got brain damage after you smashed my head on the fireplace.'

'Hey you grabbed me; I pushed you away, that was all. You tripped on a bottle and fell. I never meant for it to happen. It was an accident, they happen.'

'Because of your stupidity! Don't you realise that? Can't you get that into your thick skull,' Dylan tapped his head, instantly regretting it as it shook his already rattled brain. He turned and headed back along the landing.

'I said I'm sorry! Please don't be like this bro . . .'

'I know you can't, but I just want you to leave!'

'Say Dyl?'

'What?' Dylan bit back.

'What did you call Lucy to make them mad at you? You never mentioned it in the pub.'

Dylan stopped, 'I called her a slut. I called my own daughter a *fucking* slut. That's what makes me a bastard.' Dylan turned and left, leaving Lennon to stew on the landing on his lonesome.

Downstairs, Kirsty and Lucy moved towards him to check the bruise on his head, which over the hours had formed a large bulging bump on the right hand side of his skull. She kissed his cheek. He noticed that she'd cleared away the beer bottles and attempted to sponge away the splodge of Lennon's internal juices and wasted beer that he'd spilled out onto the carpet.

'Your bump's raised. That's a good thing,' she told him.

'Why's that a good thing?'

'It means the pressure isn't building inside your head and pressing against your brain.'

'Still hurts.'

'Here, Dad,' Lucy handed her father two little white tablets and a fresh glass of water, 'Mum says they'll help take the edge off.' She smiled like the little girl he hoped she always would be.

He never wanted Lucy to grow up; he always wanted her to be his little sweetness and nothing more. When she was one, he'd lay on the floor and Little Luce would toddle over and lift up his t-shirt and blow raspberries on his stomach. Strangely obsessed with his bellybutton, she would broggle it with her tiny inquisitive fingers, bringing Dylan into fits of rapturous giggles. From the age of four onwards, whenever he came in through the front door from work,

Lucy would always without fail rush off and grab her old man a beer. He taught her to ride a bike, fish and start a campfire. She used to be a right little tomboy. Then she discovered make-up and boys. Soon he'd lost his best little friend forever to the short road to adulthood. He looked to the future; to days he knew he could smile on; when she graduates university, the day she gets married, and the moment she passes her first child to him. Although these days seemed years away, he knew they would rush upon him like a tidal wave of euphoria. With the knowledge that the crowd outside weren't exactly showing signs of friendliness, Dylan Keene knew that he'd have to fight for the future days. No matter what blood needed spilling. He'd kill for his family; he'd assured himself of that as a fact.

Dylan took the tablets from his daughter and popped them in his mouth.

'These better not be laxatives,' he said before a swallow of water. Lucy smiled.

'One is, the other was a Viagra.'

'How would you know about Viagra?'

'I'm not child, Dad. I know a lot of things that you think I don't know about.'

'I don't even want to begin to know what you know about Luce.'

Lucy smiled, she beamed in fact. They had found a common ground of understanding. She knew things that he didn't know she knew. She was growing up. It was a fact that he'd have to learn to deal with, not her. He was the one with the problem. One day she'd get married and he'd have to let go forever. What they'd been through the last few days was just the first finger of letting go of his daughter's hand before she went out into the world on her own. Boys were only part of him letting go.

'Dad, what you said the other night, I have forgiven you. I know why you said it. I understand. But I just wanted you to know that I'm okay. He was the first boy I've. . .'

'Lucy, right now, that is the least of my worries. And even if it was at the top of my priorities, I still want to be spared the gory details. I just don't want to know. You're a girl turning into a fine young woman, and there's some things that you're just going to have to discover by yourself. Whether they hurt you or not, it will be up to you to make your own mistakes. Just remember that your mother and I will always love you.'

'Thanks Dad . . . friends?'

'Sure . . . why not!'

Lucy surged forward for a hug, as did Kirsty.

'What you said to Lennon. I think you said the right thing. It has to be said.'

'I know Kirst; I had to be the one to say something before my head popped. As much as it pained me, he needs to be told he's a disappointment in my eyes. I can't have him messing up all the time. I know he's a fuck-up. Pardon my French, but I'm sick of it.'

Kirsty smiled, so did Lucy.

'Breakfast?' Kirsty asked, 'We've still got a few eggs left.'

'I don't think I could stomach much but I'll try,' Dylan replied, and his womenfolk broke the embrace.

It wasn't long before Kirsty rustled up breakfast of eggs, beans and toast. They laid out a place for Lennon, called him but he never came. So they finished breakfast in relative peace and harmony. No awkwardness, no dirty jokes, just a normal family breakfast as the situation would allow.

Afterwards Lennon came downstairs to an air of unease. Everybody avoided eye contact fearing each other's awkward gazes. He said nothing, ignored the breakfast laid out for him and instead he snatched up the baseball bat from the table then rushed back through to the living room. Then they heard a jangle of keys being lifted and the living room door slam shut. Everybody immediately thought the worst. A heavy thump followed by a rain of smaller thumps resonated from the hallway.

Dylan shot Kirsty a warning glance and jumped up, spilling his coffee as he knocked away the table. The living room door was shut, even as Dylan reached it and tried the handle he knew it would be locked. Lennon must have blocked it with the bookcase that stood in the hallway, bracing it against the stairs.

'Lennon! What are you doing mate?' Dylan called, banging on the door.

'I'm getting out of here! You guys don't want me, and I don't want to be here trapped in this atmosphere. I can't stand it! I'm off to get help.'

'Len, there isn't anybody else. It's just us. Please, just stay here until this blows over,' Dylan pleaded. On the other side of the door, the tinging sound of a screw hit the floor. Then another.

'We both know that isn't going to happen. We have to do something. Somebody has to do something. And that person's going to be me.'

'Lennon, don't open that door. I'm warning you . . .'

'Too late bro. I'll be back soon. I'll bring beer . . .'

On the other side of the door, Dylan heard the clunk and click of the front door opening, then after a second of trepidation, it closed with a slackened bang.

Bone, Hair, Teeth

Whilst Dylan kicked and pounded at the hallway door, Kirsty and Lucy moved to the front window. All outside faces remained fixed on the young girl, staring mindlessly, vacant, empty. The essence of time sped up, whilst the feel of it seemed to slow to a treacle crawl. The gears of reality were moving too fast for their minds to comprehend. Their bodies allowed the adrenalin to gush freely into their bloodstreams to give them the ability to cope with what they were about to see.

A crunching thud resonated from outside, something along the lines of a stiletto being stamped hard into the flesh of a watermelon, a quick, thick slurping sound. Kirsty and Lucy gasped, covering their mouths with their hands.

'Oh my God! Dylan!'

'What?' asked Dylan wide-eyed, moving from the door and over to his wife's side.

'He's killed one. Lennon killed somebody!'

Dylan looked through the side pane of the bay window as a body fell back, a waterfall of fresh blood falling from the side of the man's face. It had been a paramedic once, now a ghoulish mannequin felled by the toothy screw in the end of the baseball bat. Lennon stood on the front step of the house, his chest heaving a breath that threatened hyperventilation.

Lennon swung, de-braining another member of the crowd, a sickening thud then a woman wearing a pretty floral dress slumped down onto the driveway beside Lennon, her blood jumping out of her in a spurting stream, ruining the delicate garment.

'Tell him to stop!' Lucy yelled a plea to her parents, banging violently on the window.

'Len, get back inside now!' Dylan screamed with a bite of his mouth as he fumbled with the window latch. Locked, no key! Kirsty had taken them out as a security precaution.

Lennon launched the bat again, this time bringing it down atop the head of a boy no older than sixteen. The young lad shivered into a spasm as his skull was caved in, then dropped to the floor, a thick line of blood holding contact with the spike at the end of the bat as

Lennon removed it from the boy's bashed crown. His legs quivered as synapses in his brain were cruelly put out, struggling to realise that they'd been interrupted indefinitely in their control of his central nervous system.

Dylan tried to catch Lennon's eye, the maniacal glare impenetrable by the brotherly bond that was fading between them. Whether or not he chose to ignore him, Lennon had more pressing matters to attend to.

'Key! Now!' Dylan barked at his wife. Kirsty span round and grabbed the key from off the mantelpiece, pressing it into her husband's clammy hand. His fingers had started to shake as he fumbled the key into position. He found purchase, pushing the sliver of metal in with his thumb, flipped the lock up and pushed the window open onto the back of the still standing paramedic, who staggered forward within a few feet of Lennon. With the window fully open, the stench of the crowd hit Dylan fully. Sweat was underlying, as with any group of closely packed people it was a given. But other smells offended his olfactory sense. Urine, it stung his eyes, the overpowering stench of human waste as the various members of the crowd had evacuated their bowels whilst standing still.

'Lennon, get back inside, NOW!' Dylan boomed, reaching outside the window.

His brother ignored this order; instead, he swung again with the bat, caving the head of Malcolm Jefferies, the retired milkman from five doors up. Mr Jefferies didn't fall straight away, instead he staggered left, instinctively trying to hold himself up against the car bonnet; he sat there, then turned back to the window to gaze soullessly at Lucy. His head swayed and wobbled as his blood pressure dropped. A trickle of thick dark blood dribbled down his neck as he bled out from his right ear.

'Lennon, please stop!' Dylan pleaded, 'you don't have to do this!'

Lennon ignored every word.

Noticing the car keys wrapped around his little finger, Dylan now realised that his brother was cutting a path through to the car, batting violently through the mass of bodies.

Lennon raised the bat up high, poised to swing, and then paused. A little girl before him had turned her head towards him, the only one of the crowd to break their gaze from Lucy voluntarily. She was dressed in a marigold coloured dressing gown and furry duck feet slippers. Tiny pink bows were interwoven and tied into tight bunches that sprouted like seedlings from the side of her head.

Dylan, Kirsty and Lucy watched as Lennon's face crumbled into tears. The sheer realisation of what he'd done had struck him like a bolt of lightning. He'd murdered fellow human beings in cold blood. Innocents, they'd caused no harm to hair on anyone's head, shed no blood nor shown any sign of violence or malice. They'd just been in the way, threatening an invasion into the personal bubble. But there was no explanation for what was going on. No logical argument could explain the nature of this strange crowd. Lennon shook his head, tears melted through the freckles of blood on his cheeks as the futility of it all dawned on him. He dropped to his knees; the adapted screw-in-bat fell from his grasp, unable to roll away to freedom because of the spiky protrusion.

Dylan reached out to his brother, 'Please Len, come back inside. It'll be okay.'

Lennon finally turned his gaze to Dylan and the rest of his family. 'You forgive me for fucking up?'

'Yes,' the three inside said in urgent unison.

Lennon smiled, and wiped away the tears with his wrist, smearing the blood into weepy streaks across his face. The little girl who stood before Lennon, who'd turned her strange gaze towards him seconds before he was ready to kill her, reached her little arm out and touched him lightly on the head with her minute fingers. What happened next made everybody jump back. Even as Dylan rewound and played the event over and over in the hours that followed afterwards, he still couldn't make sense of what he had seen, no matter how he tried to comprehend.

The little girl leant forward, index and middle finger outstretched; Lennon hadn't seen her move until the last moment when her tiny, gentle fingers stroked his temple. He'd said something, but it was lost in the bursting noise that followed, so Dylan never heard his brother's final words.

They didn't see the blood coming; it hit the window in a gush, their faces (insiders and outsiders) and the living room carpet like a rapid nano-wave from an exploding star. It felt like a wet slap, unusually hot and coppery. There had been a popping sensation, Dylan even felt the force of the blast touch heavily on his cheeks. Aghast, using the ends of his wrists, Dylan cleared the blood from his eyes, his brother's blood. Lennon's body was still crouched down, headless, spurting what life force remained inside of him out of his neck like a fountain. The torn white root of his spinal cord stuck out of the gushing wound, the car keys remained gripped tight in his hand, the shiny silver becoming engulfed with the flurry of blood that cascaded down Lennon Keene's shaking body. His hands were outstretched as if to say *What? What have I done?*

'Len? Len? He . . . he's . . . gone,' Dylan managed to whimper only hearing his voice inside his head. Kirsty cried out, as did Lucy. Horrible mournful cries that Dylan didn't hear as his ears were still popping with tinnitus after the force of the blast.

What was the word?

What was the word?

Human something. Spontaneous . . . Human . . . Combustion. Was that it? He'd seen part of a documentary about it once. Did it really happen? The little girl with pink bows had done this, Lennon hadn't; it had been her. She'd caused this.

The little girl's once pleasant face was now awash with Lennon's blood, it diluted the whites of her eyes, which were now back fixed on his shrieking daughter. As were the voided expressions of the surrounding crowd. Every face within a ten-foot radius was decorated with a ghoulish splattering of crimson face paint, reiterating the fact they were now a tribe, besieging the remaining Keenes in their home.

Despite her screaming tears, Kirsty took charge; someone had to. Lucy had collapsed to the floor in breathless hysterics whilst Dylan had started screaming obscenities at the blood stained girl. He was halfway from climbing out of the window with a fist clenched into a tight ball of skin, bone and vengeance, when Kirsty grabbed him by his blood-slickened shoulders and tried to pull him back. The little girl took a step forward, index and middle finger outstretched towards Dylan's forehead. Kirsty lifted a foot and shoved it against the sill. With a guttural heave, she reined her husband back in, reached forward and slammed the window shut, falling back onto the carpet in a jumble of hot slick gore and gushing red tears, just as the little girl pressed her blood slick fingers up against the glass. She pressed her hand flat against the pane and looked inside the house, blinking once. Tiny flecks of pink brain and blood stained bone seeped slowly down the smooth glass, spreading the red sheet further over the expanse of the window. The blood filled, staring eyes of the little girl peered over the edge of the sill and through the translucent curtain of gore, every shred of innocence and trust now lost from the child's cherubic expression.

Dylan was shivering and shaking his head, every second or so he'd roar with rage, punching his fists into the carpet. Lucy was now in a ball, curled up as tight as a foetus, rocking back and forth, head shaking, muttering, 'No, no, no, no, no . . .' with a bloody thumb wedged in her mouth. Her teeth bit down on her own digit.

Kirsty stood up and watched as the mass of crowd all took a step forward to take the places of the fallen, standing on bodies, to get closer to the house. Blood-wet, once familiar faces pressed up against the glass, where fragments of Lennon's bone, hair and teeth had stuck fast like chewed up and regurgitated fleshy lumps of watermelon.

The queue had gotten a little shorter, but the crowd was still the same.

THE GIRL WITH THE ELECTRIC EYES

Dylan spent the day blood stained and catatonic. The crowd outside showed more emotion than he could have managed. Slumped in the expanse of the bay window, back against the radiator, he stared at the space between his feet with eyes as wide as the Starers.

Lucy stopped crying about an hour after the Lennon incident, Kirsty brought her daughter a glass of water to soothe her parched throat from all the screaming she had put herself through. Dylan's glass remained as still as a millpond beside him.

'What are we gonna do, Mummy?' Lucy asked, pathetic and weak, her eyes pools of shimmering anguish. She hadn't called her mummy in years and seemed to genuinely mean it. Kirsty didn't dwell on the fact.

'We should get cleaned up and just keep calm until help arrives, that's what your father would want.' Kirsty looked over at her prone husband; the blood had dried near black on his face. As he had been closest to the *blast,* as it were, Dylan Keene had taken the force of his brother's head exploding. Now his face resembled a macabre death mask, the crimson paint still drying.

'But what if help doesn't come?'

'We won't know that until they arrive sweetie,' Kirsty tried her best to comfort Lucy.

'But what if help never comes? What if it's just them and us? Forever?'

'Let's get cleaned up first, then we'll decide what's next.'

Lucy pushed the living room door open as far as she could whilst her mother, armed with a broom handle adorned with a steak knife, wedged it through the gap between the door and jamb. From here, she managed to dislodge the bookcase and push its weight away from the door. Within a minute, they were in the hallway.

The front door was closed but not locked.

Beloved and unread books lay scattered on the floor; amongst the various tomes were the screws that had held the front door firm.

Seeing as Lennon had taken the front door keys with him attached to the car keys, Kirsty took it upon herself to replace the screws in their rightful place, ensuring the false safety of the house once more. She couldn't get them all the way home but she tried her best.

Kirsty and Lucy took it in turns to take showers whilst the other kept a check on Dylan. They changed clothes, brushed their teeth and hair, doing their best to remove every trace of Lennon's dark DNA from their person. They could do nothing for the startling images etched forever into their minds.

After boiling the kettle and grabbing some flannels, Kirsty and Lucy cleaned Dylan as he sat slumped and forlorn in the bay window bleeding his brother's blood onto the carpet. As he'd been topless all morning, the majority of the gore was caught in his chest and head hair, as well as encrusted to his stubbly face in dark congealing islands. He didn't protest or barely blink when they changed his jeans. Kirsty binned the blood-crusted denims. They dressed him in jogging pants and a baggy t-shirt, as these were the easiest to pull on him. When they were done, they pulled him away from the window, leaving him laid in the centre of the room, staring blankly at the ceiling, where he continued his catatonic protest.

Kirsty stroked the side his face, 'Darling, you talk when you're ready okay? No rush. We're not going anywhere.' Kirsty smiled then leant in and kissed Dylan's head. A brief taste of Lennon's coppery scent remained about Dylan's person. Kirsty wiped her lips with the back of her hand. It did little to remove the memory from her mouth.

'What do we do now, Mum?' Lucy asked.

She sighed, 'I don't know, read a book?'

'I couldn't read a book if I tried. I'm too tense. I need to do something.'

'Sleep?'

'Too wired to sleep, I need to keep active.'

Kirsty shrugged and looked at the window. The staring faces looked back, blank and inhuman, their expressions revealing nothing about the character that the faces once belonged to. Not anger nor hate, just an A-type, blank field of eyes, nose and a mouth. Without malice, without humour, without anything.

'I want to experiment.' Kirsty said with a grin, 'Get me a wire coat hanger.'

Lucy narrowed her eyes in distrust, 'Why?'

'Just an experiment. Coat hanger, now!'

Lucy gave a devilish smile then ran upstairs, returning with a coat hanger. In the meantime, Kirsty had moved back over to the window and carefully opened it to the next setting. The window was open half an inch but still secure from the latch.

Lucy handed her mother the wire coat hanger. Kirsty took it and started undoing the twists that held the hook together, straightening it out the best she could.

'What'll this prove?' Lucy asked, moving closer to her mother.

'I don't know. Let's find out.'

Kirsty threaded the straightened wire through the gap between the window and pane, over the head of the deadly little girl, and towards the blood-stained bearded man behind her. She couldn't bring herself to harm the little girl, despite what she'd done to Lennon.

The wire snaked towards his face as Kirsty threaded it further out the window.

'What you gonna do? Poke him in the face?'

'No, the eye,' Kirsty responded, 'It's a natural human reaction to blink. If they don't blink, we know that they're no longer human, or at least in control of their faculties.'

'That doesn't make sense, what if an alien has taken over them, y'know like a worm that burrows into your head while you sleep.'

'I don't think that's what's happened darling,' Kirsty paused her advancement of the wire, briefly fearful that the Starers would pull the window open without warning and snatch her from out of the living room whilst her attention was diverted. She flickered her gaze between her questioning daughter and the vulnerable window.

'Why not?'

'Because we're still compus mentis, are we not? Why hasn't your worm made a nest in our heads?'

'Err . . .'

'If they blink, it means that at least a shred of humanity still exists inside of them. They should still have basic human reactions, pain, reacting to temperatures, etcetera and so on.'

'Makes sense.'

'Good, let's see what happens.'

Kirsty threaded the wire closer and closer to the bearded man's left eye. Both deep in concentration with their breath held tight in their lungs, tying alveoli into bloodless knots, the pair of them shrieked when a hand jumped out and grabbed Kirsty by the wrist, clamping tight.

'Don't even think about it,' he said hoarsely.

Kirsty and Lucy turned, to face the owner of the hand. Dylan glared down upon them gravely, a vein in his hand popped up like a meaty worm as he held Kirsty's wrist as tight as he could without hurting her.

'If what that little girl did to Len is applicable to all of them, then you're about to make a terrible mistake.'

'What do you mean?' Kirsty replied, strangely fearful of her husband's gnarled and grisly tone.

'The wire is metal; metal conducts electricity and heat extremely well. The way Lennon died must have involved at least one of them.'

Kirsty pondered for a second. She looked at her daughter who simply shrugged, then back at Dylan.

'What do you suggest? I want to see if they still have human reactions.'

'Wait here.' Dylan headed into the kitchen, a cupboard banged then he returned wearing pink marigolds on each hand. 'Insulation,' he said knowingly.

Dylan took the wire from his wife's hand and took position by the window, then began to thread the wire towards the bearded man's face. Closer and closer, until the wire was barely an inch from the guy's left eye. Blood had crusted on his eyelashes. Dylan looked closer and could even see thin streaks of blood decorating the white of his eyeball. He hadn't even blinked when Lennon's head had exploded in front of him. Dylan pushed forward, the end of the wire jabbed into the jellied flesh of the eyeball, indenting and threatening to pop the delicate lens. Still, he didn't blink or falter his gaze from off Lucy. The guy was plainly obsessed with his daughter, and not even a needle to the eye would curb his fascination with her. Ominous light blue electricity danced along the length of the wire and towards Dylan's hand. Fearing further reaction, he drew the wire back in and closed the window. The electricity was pulled back into the Starer's eye. Almost immediately, Lucy gasped.

'Look,' she pointed outside, her voice bound by a cautious whisper, 'the little girl's eye!'

Dylan dropped the coat hanger wire next to the radiator and looked down following the direction of his daughter's finger.

The blood-stained little girl with bows in her hair, the very one who'd laid that deadly hand upon Lennon's head, had a problem with her left eye. Dylan bent low and peered into her dumb, peaceful gaze. Something flashed, ever so brief, but it remained etched on his brain. It flashed again, a tiny snap of blue lightning behind her eye, giving clues to whatever storms that raged inside her head.

The flash came again, this time green electricity circled around her pupil like a positively charged whirlpool. The colour snapped to red, then black, white, purple then back to green. Looking up, Dylan could see that every member of the crowd had the same affliction, but only in the left eye.

That confirmed it for Dylan; he was dealing with a hive mind. Many bodies controlled by a single source.

One by one, the electricity faded in the crowd's eyes, and all was relatively peaceful with the mass of bodies once again.

'They're all connected somehow . . .'

'What do you mean?' Kirsty asked.

'I poked one in the eye, but they all felt it in the same place. Did you see their eyes?'

Both Kirsty and Lucy nodded in unison.

'They are legion, for they are many,' Dylan muttered.

'What's that?' Kirsty asked, confused.

'A stupid quote from somewhere, can't remember. Probably a TV show.'

'You want to call them Legion?'

'I still prefer The Starers, a little bit more apt.'

Kirsty turned back to the crowd outside and slipped an arm round Lucy and kissed the side of her head.

'If they're plugged into the mains, can't we just throw water on them and short circuit them?' Lucy theorised.

'Can't see it working. Every human has a miniscule amount of electricity in them. It's what keeps the heart beating. Besides, we'd need a fire truck.'

'Can't we at least try? We know they're electric.'

'Sure but do it from upstairs,' Dylan warned, 'I don't want any more surprises.'

Lucy nodded and smiled grimly, then ran upstairs.

'What if they all explode? The glass . . . it could . . .' Kirsty asked.

'Then they explode,' Dylan responded, 'an idea is an idea. It beats sitting round until we starve to death.'

A rattle came from upstairs, like Lucy was removing the plastic bucket from the bathroom swing bin. Then came the sound of taps being turned on and rushing water collapsing into a hollow space. The water stopped and Lucy's footfall carried across the ceiling above their heads.

A second passed, then Dylan and Kirsty watched as a cascade of water splashed down on the closest row of the crowd near the front door.

Nothing happened.

No electrical storm, no epic splattering of blood and guts erupting against the window. Nothing.

'Oh my God!' Lucy gasped from upstairs. The black bucket fell from the upstairs window, landing squarely on the head of an elderly woman. It rattled around, before settling still. The old woman made no attempt to remove her newly acquired headwear.

'What is it sweetie?' Kirsty called.

'The crowd, they're moving . . .'

Dylan and Kirsty looked at each other for the briefest of heartbeats then stormed upstairs.

THE FIRST MOVEMENT

Out on the playing field, the crowd was on the move, spilling into the middle of the crater, swallowed up as they left the Keene's line of sight. Some hung around the edges, staring at their feet. Her parents joined Lucy by the open landing window. Lennon's Zippo remained on the windowsill. Dylan let it be, he didn't want any mementos of his brother haunting his pockets.

'What do you think they're doing?' Lucy asked.

'Not a clue, but it can't be good.'

The hundred-strong crowd had taken their gaze from off the house and now crouched down, concentrating on the burnt grass and soil at their feet.

'Maybe they've lost interest?' Kirsty pondered.

'Doubtful . . . but.' Dylan left the girls by the window and headed towards his bedroom. Crouching down by the bedside cupboard on his side of the bed, he began raving through the collection of objects.

A *Carson Ryder* novel he never finished.

An empty condom box.

A half-squeezed tube of Bonjela.

Long dead batteries.

A murky stolen/liberated pint glass.

A pair of military green binoculars.

Dylan ignored everything else, grabbed the binoculars, and headed back for the landing. Raising the eyepiece to his eyes he looked out across the crowd.

Scanning across the sea of faces staring up at him, he soon fixated his gaze on the crater in the middle of the playing field and the crowd that remained gathered there.

What he saw chilled him.

Fingers breaking against aged rocks in the soil.

What Lucy had said earlier was now coming true. The crowd they could see gathered outside by the crater were digging into the ground at their feet with bare hands, scrambling into the baked and burnt earth using fingernails as shovels. Some scraped dirt back towards them, whilst others pushed it along with the side of their hands. A plume of dirty brown dust had started to rise above the prone crowd as they moved earth to and fro. There must've been more at the bottom of the crater.

'What are they doing?' Kirsty asked.

'They're digging.'

'What?'

'They're digging, with bare hands.'

'Like my dream?' Lucy added, followed by an audible dry swallow.

'Yeah.'

'That's bad.'

'It's not good.'

'What are they digging for?' Kirsty asked.

'That would be the obvious question,' Dylan replied with an annoyed rasp, 'I can't see for the crowd!'

'What comes next sweetie? In your dream I mean.' Kirsty asked.

'Fire I think, I see lots of fire.'

'Ahh, screw this!' Dylan rasped and moved down the other end of the landing. Reaching up he grabbed the cord for the loft hatch and pulled it down. With the flick of a catch, the metal ladders descended down. Taking the binoculars with him, Dylan barged up the steps and into the attic.

'Dylan, where are you going?'

'Assessing the damned situation!'

The attic lights flicked on, and an instant later came a crashing sound.

'Christ, Dyl what are you doing up there?'

He didn't respond. More noise, the tearing of fabric and heavy tiles sliding off the roof. One smashed on the driveway outside. Lucy looked out. It had missed one of the Starers by mere inches.

Kirsty headed for the loft space. Climbing the ladder, she poked her head over the opening to see Dylan bracing himself on the roof trusses, kicking the roof tiles off from the inside.

'Have you lost it?'

'Maybe,' he said between kicks.

'You're fucking up our roof, how much is this going to cost to repair?'

Dylan paused from kicking in the felt, his eyebrows rose, widening his eyes incredulously. 'You really think money matters anymore? It doesn't; we've long left behind tax codes, overdrafts and futile wishes for lottery wins. Life has changed. Things have fucking changed!'

'Has Dad lost his marbles?' Lucy asked from the bottom of the ladder.

'He's lost something.' Kirsty bit her lip and turned, giving her daughter a wry, trying smile. Then she turned back to Dylan. Daylight poured in through the roof.

'So what's life about now?' Kirsty asked her husband, now questioning his sanity.

'Survival,' came his one word answer; then he vanished through the gap in the roof.

'Wait!' Kirsty called, but his legs slithered through like frightened snakes and she was left alone in the attic with boxes of junk and the dried up corpses of spider shells.

With shaking fingers, Dylan pulled his way up to the ridge of the roof. Straddling the rooftop, he had a better vantage point from there. He could see for miles. He raised the binoculars to his face again. The digging crowd remained focused on their work, the rest of them kept clear of the centre as if they'd become drone sentinels of a sacred place. Mounds of dirt had started to build up at the edges of the burnt circle where mindless hands had pushed soil out of the way of progress. A few, but not many, had used some base primal initiative and started using scraps of wreckage as makeshift shovels.

What the hell were they digging for? Dylan thought. Something on the plane, a black box maybe?

He moved the binoculars round, following a new horizon that he couldn't have seen before. It pretty much told the same story. People everywhere. From this vantage point, he could see over the roof of the bus, the Old Man who had been waiting in the rain was still standing, staring at the house. His face was ghostly white, cheeks drawn down as if he were a melting candle. Behind the Old Man, Dylan recognized the Ladlow kid from down the road, the only time he'd ever seen the Ladlow kid out and about was in his wheelchair, crippled up and bent within himself, arms and fingers locked with some grim representation of a clawing tree branch. Now he was standing up across the road, still a little bent over, but dribble-free regardless.

Up the entire length of Westfield Road, bodies were pressed in against each other. At one point, he thought he had seen his best mate Harry Price amongst the collage of faces, but when he scanned back to find his ginger bearded friend, he had become lost along with the rest of them. The next street was much the same, as was Manton

Drive behind them. People's gardens, fishponds, a few individuals on shed roofs, all the same. In a few bedroom windows, Dylan would see a figure standing eerily behind the glass, looking out towards him, trapped by the strange purpose that pushed people towards his house and their own four walls. Even the fields that surrounded the town looked to be crammed with people. There seemed to be no letting up in finding a break in the crowd.

It was endless.

It was hopeless.

. . .

No . . .

Everything has to end sometimes.

Hope always resides somewhere, even in the dark pits of despair, you'll find diamonds in the mire, doom wasn't always certain when you were staring death in the face. Jews escaped the concentration camp at Auschwitz; passengers sometimes survived even the most horrific plane crashes. Didn't a stewardess survive falling out of a plane sometime in the seventies? People survived the Titanic, the Twin Towers, tsunamis and earthquakes, but this was different.

Hope was there; he just couldn't see it yet.

It was out there somewhere in the ether, beyond the touch of his fingertips. Hope was waiting for an opportunity. Dylan prayed that it didn't wait too long to show its head.

Dylan removed the binoculars from his eyes and gave a fateful sigh, dropping his head down to his chest. He picked at a piece of dry moss on the next ridge tile, compacted it between his fingers and flicked it off the roof. He didn't see where it landed. The field of faces gazed back, their heads fixed in a position that looked upon a point a few feet below him.

Lucy.

It was all about her.

But why?

Nothing made sense.

Not the crowd, not Lennon's death. It seemed that whatever happened next could either provide answers or encourage more questions that are endless. Dylan shook his head and flicked some more moss off the roof and into the crowd, longing for a machine gun and a helicopter.

And a pilot.

And a million quid.

And a beer.

And Lennon.

Dylan looked across to the Loughery's home. He thought about the need for more supplies should things get dire, but the distance was too far to jump. The Mercers' on the other side was easily reachable. They'd gone abroad, their third holiday this year, so at least the house would be secure should he have to smash his way in through the roof to get in for supplies. He giggled at the thought of discovering his neighbours' secrets. What things did they hide away in drawers and stuffed at the back of cupboards.

Old love letters?

Compromising photos?

Illegal pharmaceuticals?

Ill-gotten gains?

He could get into the Mercers, should things start to get dire and they needed more food. Maybe from the Mercer's he could jump to the next house. This comforted him somewhat. His house was an island, but at least he could hop to the next isle.

Dylan sighed again, closed his eyes tight and enjoyed the silence and the sun on the side of his face, trying not to cry at the futility of it all. He imagined a faraway beach, palm trees, Mai Tai's, the dreamer's tropical paradise. A sunset burned through far skies; a fading, shimmering glow that just screamed the end of a perfect day. Kirsty was with him, slimmer, like when he first met her. Lucy is always smiling, she reads now, thinking of becoming an artist just like her old man wanted to be before the real world demanded that he pay bills by working a shite twelve hour a day job. Lennon's there as well, he's with Jessica Wrent, an old girlfriend that broke up with him because he got too wasted all of the time. They only went out for a month, but at the time, Dylan and Kirsty thought they made a cute couple, as they liked most of the same things.

His mind wandered over to potential band names Lennon, Harry and he had considered briefly in the past.

The Caution Horses.

The Gallivants.

Thirteen Miles to Nowhere.

Sunshine Sitdown.

Attempted Murder of Krows, (AMOK for short.)

They all disagreed on one or another. It seemed that they would go on being the great nameless and un-gigged.

'You came up here to sunbathe?'

Dylan opened his eyes, and the faraway sunset died. Kirsty's severed head was sat on the rooftop staring at him. She looked paler than in the dream, a pasted ghost of her former bright and cheerful self.

Worn was the word.

'Eh?' he asked the disembodied head.

'You look like you're sunbathing. You ruined our roof to sunbathe?'

'It looks that way.'

'Can I join you?'

'Sure, just be careful.'

The severed head grew shoulders and arms, followed by a full body as his wife was carefully born out of the hole in the roof. Kirsty scrambled up towards him. He grabbed her hand to steady her and she sat down next him.

'Just needed to get some fresh air and sunshine y'know?'

Kirsty looked around the rooftop, seemingly admiring the view. He doubted it.

'Yeah. It's nice up here. I see why you came up.'

'Just looking for a way out of all this.'

'And?'

'Nothing yet. I'll let you know.'

'Do you want to talk about Lennon?'

'No, not yet. No need to try and comprehend it. No point. It's too bizarre to even get my head round.'

'You guys better not be doing anything gross up there!'

Lucy's severed head appeared from the roof hole. Without asking or caring for permission, she climbed out and up the tiles, sitting in-between them.

'Nice view. If you like crowds,' Lucy commented dryly.

'Lucy, be quiet,' her mother urged. 'Let's just sit and be together.'

Lucy sighed but didn't protest. Although none of them wanted to admit it, time was running out for them to spend as a family. Whether they died of starvation, dehydration or just plain old stabbed each other to death in a furious fit, only the coming days would tell.

Lucy put both her arms around her parents' shoulders. Despite the numbness they felt in their minds and their bodies, they sat like precarious birds upon the roof for what seemed like hours, watching as one by one the streetlights flicked on an angry red, the only people they knew of watching the sun fall through the fading calm of a darkening purple evening sky. Fifty miles away, just beyond where the curvature of the great earth stole the horizon away from the sight of the common man, a black cloud raged and rolled into itself, a brimming, swollen sack of soaked cotton, edging towards them, faster than usual storms, but not uncommon. Rain, thunder and lightning were by-products of this undulating mass. It was bringing it all to them, softening the ground, making it easier for bare but eager fingers to dig.

The three rooftop dwellers spared no thoughts on this coming weather pattern, for their minds were set on hope, whether it be helicopters with high calibre machine guns or a rescue party bringing respite from over the crowd filled horizon. They all wished, yearned and prayed to whatever god was listening that somebody was coming.

Unbeknownst to them, somebody was.

Hole 'Lotta Trouble Going On

They watched the sunset, then after climbed down off the roof in a haze. Content would be a strange way to describe their subdued nature, considering the circumstances, but they all appeared calm and collected, seemingly resigned to whatever fate awaited them.

Kirsty started making an evening meal, cooking the last of the meat they had and the few remaining vegetables. She threw a tin of tomatoes on top and the meal was ready. It was food. If they were to give it a name, it would probably be called apocalypse stew or some other ironic moniker.

Halfway through dishing it up, the lights went out with a click, as the fuse box was denied its flow of electricity. Dylan sat down at the table and started to eat with the last gleam of twilight for illumination.

'We knew it was coming. No point getting worked up about it.' Dylan shrugged.

'But what if . . .' Kirsty said peering at her husband in the fading light.

'But what if nothing, we can't stop the inevitable.' Dylan shovelled a forkful of broccoli into his mouth and chewed knowingly. 'The water will be next. After tea we'll make sure every container is brimming.'

Kirsty sat down dutifully and ate in silence. Lucy played with her food, eating as slowly as she could, if at all. Eventually, long after her parents had finished theirs, Lucy devoured every morsel. Despite not feeling hungry, she knew there was a good chance that food would soon become scarce over the next few days. The time to eat was now.

After they all had finished eating, Dylan checked to make sure every single container was filled with water, drinking down as much as his already full stomach would allow. He had what would probably be his final shower, and enjoyed it, even if it was cold. He encouraged his family to do the same, as soon their house would be a desert as well as a prison. Lucy washed up once the water supplies were replenished and Kirsty dug out some tea light candles while they prepared for bed.

Dylan posted no sentry tonight, he was too tired and he didn't feel like leaving the security work up to the girls. He'd chance it, telling himself if they wanted to get in, they'd be in by now. There wasn't much point in trying to fight them. They could, but the end would come, when the end would come.

Lucy dragged her mattress into the master bedroom and dropped it at the foot of their bed.

'I'm sleeping in here tonight. No arguments,' Lucy stated, dumping her duvet on top of her new bed.

'I'm not arguing with that,' Dylan reasoned as he opened the window. The clouds above rolled slowly with turbulence as a storm brewed in the high darkness of the sky. A silent hum echoed in the air, as if the oxygen was caught in a film, or a fine gauze that stopped the molecules moving about freely. Even though he couldn't see this pressure, he could feel it pressing down on him from above.

It hurt his bruise.

Summer storms were the best. He decided to leave the curtains open so he could see the show from the comfort of his bed.

Kirsty came back from the bathroom, having completed her nightly ablutions, her hair tied up in a ponytail. Her breasts hung free beneath one of his old *Simpsons* t-shirts; Homer appeared lumpier than usual.

'We all need sleep,' Dylan said, stripping down to his jogging pants.

Lucy and Kirsty both nodded in agreement.

'If we all get a good eight hours, we'll be able to think straight in the morning, maybe think of a way out, or . . .' his voice trailed off as he even doubted himself. He shook his head and shrugged his shoulders as the words became lost. There was no way out, only the figment of time ticking away until they all met their end. Starvation or a suicide pact? These were Dylan's grim reckonings. He felt no reason to admit his predictions to his family.

'Let's just get some sleep,' he said and climbed into bed. Kirsty climbed in next to him. Lucy dropped down at the foot of the bed. Nobody said goodnight, as it wasn't going to be, they all knew that.

***

It wasn't the tumultuous rolls of thunder that woke Dylan up in the depths of the midnight hour, nor was it an arm of hot lightning punching ferociously down from the skies, splitting the branch of a tree about a mile away.

It was the rain.

When the *plop-plop-plop* started to puddle on the ceiling above his head, this quietly destroying noise eventually found its way into his head and his dreams. An image flashed through his sleep-drenched mind.

The roof.

Dylan sprung bolt upright, his back and shoulders awash with sweat, his forehead felt particularly wet. He wondered where Lennon was and his mind toiled as to where he'd last seen him. More often than not, Dylan had lost his brother on many nights out as Lennon went off on his own tangents and stumbling, clumsy missions. It pained to admit to himself that his brother was laid headless on the front driveway, the Starers using him as a welcome doormat.

A drop of moisture balled by gravity beat down on top of his crown. Dylan felt his hair. It was sodden. He looked up, a small dark puddle had formed on the ceiling above his head, shivering and glistening, taking in all the light it could. Again, an image flashed through his mind.

The roof. He'd left a hole in the damned roof!

Dylan reached for the torch that he'd lain prepared on the bedside drawers and jumped off the sodden mattress, narrowly avoiding crushing Lucy as she lay at the foot of the bed. He hopped over her head and danced sideward into the hall. The attic was still open; he could feel the chill of the rain swept wind rushing in and across the landing. Dylan shivered, shrugged, then moved up the ladder to inspect the damage he'd caused.

Standing on the ladder, he could see a river of black cloud sweeping above the house. The wind had picked up since he'd retired to bed, now the northerly breeze stirred up the weather, creating the storm that now raged around his house. Splatters of rain dropped freely into the attic space, a large patch of insulation was soaked through, as were the nearby timbers. This was all his own doing and if he didn't do something about it, the ceiling would soon cave in on his family's heads with the soaking weight of the water.

Dylan descended and headed downstairs to the kitchen, where in the darkness and from memory, he dug out bin liners and duct tape from one of the drawers. Then he remembered he had the torch and clicked it on, keeping the beam low to the floor.

He stopped in the living room and viewed the dark crowd that waited outside. The Starers. All heads were slightly raised towards the sky, in truth it was his daughter that their obsessive gaze fixated on.

Lightning cracked over a distant field, briefly illuminating the crowd from behind. In unison, their eyes showed the briefest flash of blue/green. When the lightning disintegrated, the crowd's eyes returned to normal. Black and hiding in the safety of their collective shadow. Dylan shivered, except this time it wasn't the chilled air that unnerved him.

He headed back up to the attic and climbed into the space; knees aching and creaking in unison with the ply board that decked out the floor of the loft. Dylan looked up into the night sky, he dared not stick his head out the hole for two simple reasons; the fear of a lightning strike across his forehead and the continuing gaze of the Starers down below was enough to give him nightmares. Their mass of gathered faces, illuminated by the thick gloom of night was bad enough for the imagination, let alone reality.

Perched on his knees, Dylan ripped off a bin liner and tucked it into the space between the roof timbers and tiles. The wind grabbed at it, flapping the polythene like a plastic bird in the midst of a death spasm.

Grimacing from the burgeoning rain, Dylan tore off another bin liner and tucked it into the lower portion of the hole. Quickly as he could, he tore off a length of duct tape and gently sealed the gap. He used more duct tape to secure the underneath and voilà! The hole was closed. Dylan smiled, even though he had created the task by his own wrongdoing, he was pleased with what he had accomplished considering the circumstances.

'Dylan!' a voice hissed from below.

'What?' he hissed back.

'What you doing?'

'Fixing a hole.'

Kirsty's head and shoulders appeared through the loft opening. She held a tea-light on the side of a plate in one hand. As she came up through the opening, Dylan couldn't help but notice her nipples poking hard through the old skinny t-shirt she wore for bed. The penetrating rain had soaked her through as she'd lain beside him. Her hair was wet and plastered back, giving her a wide-eyed, rabbit like gaze, the torchlight glinting against the fearful whites of her eyes. A smile curled up from her cool lips.

He averted his gaze to her eyes.

'I thought you'd pissed the bed.'

'I wish I had. We'll have to change the sheets now.'

'No great shakes; you coming back to bed?' she asked, placing the tea-light on the ply board as she crawled gingerly into the loft space.

'Yeah, I've . . . err . . . made a mess of the roof, we had water pouring in.'

'I told you so. Dickhead.'

'I'm sorry, a moment of madness,' he apologised meekly.

'We all have them.'

'I'll get it fixed.'

'I don't think it matters anymore, do you?'

'No,' he admitted, trying to hold her steely gaze, but he couldn't, he was too honest. They both knew life would be over soon, a strange knowing between them told them this. They'd both accepted that death awaited them. The only question was how. Their unsaid words said it all.

'Is the world over?' Kirsty whispered.

'I don't know. I don't want it to be.'

'Me too. I feel . . . strange . . . sort of content. It's weird, like, even though the world's gone to shit, I'm happy I'm spending it with my family. I know things haven't been great, but I'm happy for what I've had. No family is perfect; we've all got our creases.'

'You sound like you're giving your own eulogy.'

Kirsty smiled and placed the tea-light down near the opening. Moving onto all fours, she crept towards him, her head bowed to one side, stalking him cat like. She gave her head a nod towards a patched portion of the roof he'd fixed.

'Would you like to fix another hole?' Kirsty breathed coyly, slinking closer.

'You didn't just say that did you? It was cheesy, you don't do cheese.'

'I did, and I want it,' she purred.

Usually it was him that did the chasing when it came to amorous attentions. Only if she was drunk or the week before her period did she ever show him any hint of sexual advances. This was a rarity. Kirsty sidled up to him and kissed his cheek. He dropped the torch;

it fell away from his fingers, and rolled across the ply, settling into a bed of insulation.

'What about Lucy?'

'She's fast on. I never knew she snored.' Kirsty gave a devilish smile, kissing him again, wetter this time. He tasted her toothpaste on his tongue.

'Are you sure?'

'I want you, *now!*' she raised her voice a little, not in volume but in intensity, speaking from the depths of her diaphragm.

'Shall we go downstairs?' he kissed her on the cheek then moved to her lips as he felt a stirring within himself. 'The sofa . . . ?'

'No . . . here,' she gasped as his lips played gentle kisses on the nape of her neck, 'now!'

'But . . . why?' he asked, then felt stupid about even questioning such an offer.

'The world . . . it's over. I don't want to be alone. I . . . need it just once more. That'll see me through. I don't want to be alone . . . just once. Please . . .'

'You think it's ended? Humanity? You really think it's all over for us?' he asked, pausing from the kisses. She continued nibbling his ears.

'Maybe, but just to be on the safe side. Give it to me Dyl. I need something. I need to feel something other than this horrible fear of whatever comes next. Don't argue.'

He took her fully on the lips, moving his hand behind her head. He ran his fingers into her hair, stroked her back, across her shoulders and down the length of her arm. They played with each other's fingers, tips dancing against one another, held hands then tried to find a position that suited the awkwardness of the situation. Standing up wasn't an option as the roof was too low (unless he stuck his head out of the hole in the roof like a tank commander). The ply board was too hard on their knees for any prolonged vigorous action, so they settled on a spoon position with her head resting on his arm whilst he embraced her with the other. With a tug, he pulled down his jogging bottoms to his knees, with another tug, Kirsty's bedtime shorts were in the same position.

She was already wet when he entered her, guiding him in by touch and the scattered dancing glows of the tea-light which cast their conjoined shadows on the belly of the roof behind them.

With the storm raging above, their daughter sleeping below, and the thousands upon thousands of strangers waiting outside for them, they shuffled together on the grainy dirt and wet wood of the attic, rutting like the doomed rare beasts that they had become. Roof spiders watched on with arachnid contempt, skittering triumphantly into their hidey-holes until their trespassers had completed their last rituals and left their domain in tidy peace.

They both finished quickly and contentedly. Whilst in the throes of a post-orgasmic tide, Kirsty whispered in his ear, 'I'm pregnant.'

Dylan couldn't comment positively about the future, nor could he doom the potential life to a dark, unknown void. No words could be formed in his mind as they both drifted away to a thankfully dreamless slumber. Dylan said nothing, him holding her tighter was answer enough, embracing until they were both falling asleep in a jumble of goose-pimpled arms and legs, remaining fixed in that cosy and content position, watching the tea-light die its fading death, until the sweet, inquisitive hum of dawn awoke them. In a way, she was happy he'd said nothing. She'd told him. It was enough that he knew. Given any other circumstance she knew he'd be happy. If and when they got out of this mess, they'd talk about it some more.

If and when.

If and when.

***

'Mum, Dad? Are you up there?'

Dylan's eyes peeled open, his arm was dead; his hip ached a stabbing sore as he began to move, making him feel old and useless, which he wasn't. Not yet. Kirsty stirred at the same time; she turned and looked at him, smiling sleepily as the last memory of last night came back to her. Was today bin day? He'd forgotten to put the bins out last night. Was it past seven? Damn.

Dylan smiled back at his wife and said, 'Lucy.'

The smiles faded and Kirsty pulled away from him, their coital secretions bonding them together in places with a dry, abrupt stickiness that pinched at their close skin. Dylan winced as he moved his legs, chafing his buttocks on the dusty ply and he pulled up his joggers to his hips. He needed reminding of why they'd slept in the attic. Kirsty adjusted herself and poked her head down through the loft opening.

'What is it sweetie?' Kirsty asked.

'What'cha doin up there?'

'Just fixing this dammed hole that your dad made, we've had rain pouring in all night.'

'I've been awake an hour, what have *you* two been doing?' a direct, probing insinuation; more than just a simple question from his curious daughter.

'Say Luce?' Dylan said, 'see if we've still got any gas, I could do with a coffee.'

'Will do *Daaad*,' Lucy chirped, then headed downstairs, causing a commotion with pots and pans.

'You think she believed us?' Kirsty turned and asked with a guilty smile.

'Not for a second.'

Kirsty gave a childish snigger then crawled forward, kissing her husband on the lips.

'You gonna have a shave today? You're getting a beard again. I've got a rash on my neck from you nuzzling me.'

'I'd rather save the water now.'

Kirsty bit her lip, looked down coyly and then back at him. 'Was last night okay?'

'The best,' he said without a beat. He reached out and stroked her arm.

'I suppose that counts for something, at least we'll die happy that we still loved each other.'

'Hey, we're not dead yet, so don't even think like that. As long as we're alive, we've got a chance. You have to believe that. It's not over until it's over.'

'I know. It just seems a chore to go downstairs and face *them*.'

'How about we keep the curtain shut, try and have a normal morning. Maybe play a board game or something?'

She smiled, 'You're shitting me? Lennon will piss his pants when he hears that!' Kirsty shook her head in disbelief at her husband's suggestion, but her expression dropped away in realisation at what she had said. She raised her hand over her mouth in vain effort to stop the words that had already left her lips.

'Oh, I'm sorry Dyly . . . I didn't mean . . .' she tried to apologise.

'It doesn't matter Kirst, don't worry about it. I've forgotten a few times myself.'

'I know he wasn't the most perfect brother to you, but we still loved him didn't we?'

'Yeah.'

'I'm sorry, Dyly. Grief does funny things to your mind. I still don't believe it. What do we do? I don't want to just leave him out there.'

'Much as I want to, there's nothing we can do. So try not to think about it. Let's just head downstairs and try and rustle up some breakfast.'

Kirsty nodded, smiled and held back the threat of tears. Then she descended the loft ladders and made her way downstairs.

'I'll be down in a minute.'

Dylan looked up. The bin bags he'd used to bung the hole in the roof hadn't lasted the night, now fresh, clear sun light filtered through the broken void. He stood, cracking his feet, popping his knees. Reluctant, he stuck his head through the roof hole. Golden early sun warmed his cheeks. The storm had cleared the air, refreshing the ozone; the blue skies promised a bright, clear day.

The Starers had been washed, though cleaner than the festering mass they were yesterday, now they looked bedraggled. Hair was either plastered to foreheads or puffed up as beautifying conditioners had been washed away with the night's storm. They looked wild. Dylan bent down and picked up the green binoculars he'd left in the attic and put them to his eyes to observe the morning crowd closer.

There was no end to them, just a continuing mass of strange plain faces staring back at him. More than a few looked emaciated as their bodies burnt away fat reserves to survive. He swung over to the circle of bodies in the field. Digging through the night, they had made progress amongst the sharp skeletons of wreckage from the plane. Those digging within the pit he couldn't see, for they were hidden by the deepening depths of the crater and the mounting mounds of soil that had built up around the circumference of the hole.

They were digging by hand, taking a clump in their hands, taking it to the end then dumping it at the edges. Then they'd return to their spot and take another handful.

Rinse and repeat.

They were like ants or worker bees, a hive mind concerned and concentrating on completing a single, main purpose

Dig.

The Diggers and The Starers. Whatever next?

Others had joined the edge of the amateur quarry, now bent over on hands and knees, pulling the gathered soil back behind to level it out, working as a tight ship to avoid the sides collapsing in on top of those in the pit.

Narrowing his gaze, Dylan could make out that some had blood dripping from their hands from where their searching fingers had collided with a hidden rock or stone, breaking nails and scoring skin in the process. He paid more attention to their hands. Some of the diggers had tips of dirty white showing beneath the mud and the blood.

Bone, Dylan thought. They're working their fingers to the bone. Yet, they carried on painless and without complaint, tendons and sinew holding their tender bones together, the only thing that stopped their hands from falling apart; a grisly, perfect workforce that any regime would be proud to enslave.

Dylan shuddered and ducked back into the attic. A vile yet empty sickness churned away inside of him. He put the binoculars down and picked up the torch he had dropped last night. The bulb had faded to dull glow, the battery flattened by lust and forgetfulness. Dropping into a sex induced sleep, he had forgotten to turn off the torch, wasting the batteries.

While Dylan worried about saving energy, a new concern became apparent to his senses that made his head jerk so fast it jarred his neck.

A scream from downstairs.

Spilt

They still had live gas. The flaming ring *sssssss'd* and burnt away the North Sea's finest by-product.

Pots and pans were scattered all over the floor, as was the water they once contained. Kirsty was in the corner of the kitchen by the twirly cupboard, crouched low, her forehead bleeding. Lucy had a pan in her hand and was holding it aloft in her hands whilst screaming at her mother.

'What the hell's going on down here?' Dylan barked at them both.

Lucy turned to face him, her brow furrowed in anger 'You should have known better. You're animals, the pair of you!'

'What the hell are you talking about Luce?' Dylan intervened.

'I asked Mum what you two got up to in that loft. She told me. Can't you have a little bit of respect? Uncle Lennon is dead and all you two want to do is fuck!'

'Lucy!' Dylan protested at her shocking foul language. She didn't look like she cared in the slightest.

'No, shut up!' Lucy raised a bread knife and pointed it at her father. It was the first time he noticed it. He felt his muscles automatically tense at the sight of the blade.

'She threw the pan at me,' Kirsty whimpered from the corner. The happy, content face that he'd woken up this morning had been replaced by one of pure primal fear. Her eyes where shockingly wide; lips tight with concern.

'You're supposed to be thinking of a way out of this! Not screwing each other's brains out.' Lucy's gaze bore a burning petulance into her father's eyes. They had the same eyes, they were equals. Dylan's returned stare didn't falter. He was worried for his daughter; but he wasn't scared of her or what she could do.

'Listen here, missy!' Dylan raised his finger and his voice to his daughter, 'We're married, that means we can want each other whenever we see fit. It's none of your damned business. Your mother needed me last night and I needed her. You have to understand that Luce . . .'

'I only told her that we'd made love. It's what married people do, you probably don't want to imagine your father and I together but it happens, you don't need to make a big deal out of it.'

'I know it happens, when I sleep over at a friend's house, I guessed that you jumped on each other straight away, but not while I'm here. It's gross.' Lucy waved the blade casually. From the look on her face she didn't even realise that she had the knife in her hand and was terrifying her parents with her unjust actions.

'Luce listen, this was different. Your mum was worried last night. The way things are going, she thought that we'd never have a chance to be together again . . . in that way.'

'I don't care! You should have some self-control, for Christ sake, you're old enough!' She jabbed the knife in the direction of Dylan's stomach. He tensed, preparing himself to fight his first born. She had a wild glaze to her eyes. He remembered her dream, wondering if she was fully aware that she was becoming dangerously close to seeing her prediction come true. He felt like grabbing his petulant daughter by the throat and screaming some sense into her face. This thought lingered for a second, then he regained control of the rash animal that made all the bad decisions, stopping it from barking back, he kept the leash on tight, reining it in.

'Lucy put down the knife.'

Lucy looked at the knife in her hand. Surprise filtered across her face. Her fingers went slack and the knife fell onto the kitchen floor, stabbing the lino then falling on its side.

'Lucy, go upstairs and leave us alone. I thought we'd put this attitude behind, I thought we'd turned a corner so we could all work together to get through this. Clearly, I was wrong. Now get out of my sight before I do something you'll regret.' He made no emphasis on the word *regret*. He did not speak it unnaturally as part of the sentence syntax nor did he alter his tone throughout. He said it coolly and with direct promise. He glared at his daughter. She got the message.

'I . . .' she stalled, looking down at the knife at her feet. She now fully grasped what she'd come close to doing.

'Go,' again, coolly, efficient even. 'I don't want to see or hear you.'

Lucy huffed once, flaring her nostrils like a mardy piglet, then stomped out. Dylan picked up the knife and placed it on the counter top then moved down to his wife, who he now noticed was holding her arm.

'She burnt me with the water.'

Dylan looked at the red raw scold on his wife's arm.

'Christ! She did this?'

Kirsty nodded.

Dylan grabbed a fresh Jay cloth from the drawer and dipped it in one of the remaining pans of water on the counter top, and then he applied it to Kirsty's arm. Naturally, she winced. He crouched down next to her, so they were both sitting in the thin puddle of water that lay like a glistening skin on the kitchen lino.

'What happened?' He asked.

'I came down stairs and she was boiling the water like you asked. She asked *"What were you two up to in the loft?"* So I told her, I said we needed to make love. Then she screamed at me and threw the pan at me. Luckily, it didn't quite have time to boil, but I jumped out of the way, knocking over the pans we had on the top. I'm sorry Dyl.'

'You had no choice, don't worry about it.'

'All we have is the bottled stuff.'

'We've still got plenty; you've only knocked over a few pans. The bath's still full and if it rains again we can fill up the pans.'

A puffing noise came to his ears, he turned and looked over to the hob. The flaming blue ring that Lucy had turned on was now choking the last remnants of gas from the pipes. The flame hissed and puffed once more before petering out. Dylan walked over and turned the knob. He knew the gas wouldn't come on again, but he wasn't taking any chances. Not today, not the way his luck was going.

'What are we going to do with her?' Kirsty looked into his eyes, she was shaking.

Dylan sighed, 'I don't know, maybe feed her to them things outside, it's clear she's the one they want.'

'You can't be serious?' Kirsty said aghast.

Dylan ignored the question; instead, he leant down and held his hand out. 'C'mon, let's sit on the sofa. It'll be comfier.'

Kirsty nodded meekly and took his hand with her good hand. Dylan pulled her out of the puddle and to her feet. Leading her to the living room, he sat her down.

'I'll get you a drink and some tablets.'

Dylan returned to the kitchen, poured a half a glass of water and popped out two Co-codamals. They still had plenty left from when he jarred his back last year. They were still in date, not that it would matter anyway. His wife was in pain, he would've given a shot of heroin if it took away the sting from that horrific burn his daughter had caused. Back in the living room, he gave them to his wife.

'Knock these back, they'll take the edge off, then I'll make you some breakfast.'

'Cheers, Dyl.' Kirsty did as she was told, dropping the tablets into her mouth, then sipped at the water. Dylan sat down next to her.

The curtains were open, the crowd outside staring in like glaring visitors at a zoo.

We're animals, Dylan thought, *nothing but trapped rats to these still monsters*.

Pieces of Lennon's head and brain remained stuck to the front window where the rain hadn't quite washed the remnants away. Flies gathered around the morsels, their tongues probing the grisly mess. It had become part of the scenery now, Dylan didn't want to dwell on it, but he had no choice.

The rest of the day sloped on in silence. Lucy upstairs, her parents below, embraced, longing for a way out away from this madness that surrounded them. Trying not to move in order to conserve energy, they hugged long into the afternoon. Sometimes they heard Lucy crying above them. Her only sympathisers were the Starers outside, who gazed upon her like relentless followers of a charismatic and enchanting deity.

They talked about Lucy a little, deciding that something had to be done in order for them to survive as long as possible without tearing each other's throats out.

Dylan didn't feel sorry for his daughter. He'd brought her up by the best of his parental abilities, both Kirsty and he had. But sometimes you just couldn't negotiate or reason with her. There didn't seem much point in helping her along if this was the way she was going to behave all the time.

Dylan did however feel sorry for the folks outside. Clearly, they had no mind on the matter, they didn't decide one day, as a group to come and stand outside his house. Other forces were at work here, a conspiracy against his family. These poor souls were lost, now mindless puppets, controlled by a force much higher than the human mind can comprehend.

Tiredness took over soon and the afternoon dragged on without the Keene's consciousness bearing down on them, for they slept embraced in each other's arms, the Starers staring in, the world turning around them all. Clouds mutated into new woolly forms, sunlight warming everything under her bright watchful eye. The world carried on as normal as it could, not much changed.

Until the fires started.

THE HOT PROMISE

The fires had continued in the pit for some time. She watched as smoke billowed up like sleeping dragons' breath from the crater that had been exploded, dug and gouged in the centre of the playing field. She couldn't see the source of the heat or smoke as the sides were too steep to see the bottom. But Lucy watched on through her father's binoculars on top of the roof, intrigued and scared at the same time. She considered informing her parents of the latest development, but decided against it. She didn't want to face them right now and besides, if they were worried about it, they'd come and get her.

The pit had grown in size since yesterday. One side had partly caved in, bringing down one of the homes whose garden backed onto the playing field. Now the diggers diligently carried bricks and timbers as well as rock and soil from the expanse of the pit.

The guilt of what Lucy had done to her mother; the burn, bore down on her, marking her face with a concerned frown that cut thin red lines into her forehead. She wanted to apologise, but didn't know how to start, shame had made her hide herself away for the day. She couldn't face her parents, they just didn't see that she lived here as well. Confusion raged within her. She wanted to say sorry, but at the same time, she was still mad at what they did. Fucking right underneath her nose! She didn't need that. Didn't they think that she'd hear them?

She'd overreacted, that was all. She'd calmed down, had time to reflect. Soon she'd go downstairs say sorry and hug them both. Hopefully that would be enough and things would be right again. It wasn't like they could ground her, was it?

Her stomach churned with waves of hunger, but she couldn't face eating a thing, for she was more entranced by what was happening in front of her.

Perched upon the ridge of the roof, basking in the delight of the sun's glow, Lucy watched through the lenses of the binoculars; several pillars of smoke rose up from the belly of the pit, rising and interweaving into a single, fuming black band. She was sure that several times, she had heard broken screams; short, agonising bursts that sounded human, yet betrayed everything she had heard before.

Even up high, she could smell the crowd. A collection of human vapours assaulted her senses, but she soon became accustomed to it. The still atmosphere held the foul ether in the air before her. She longed for even the slightest of zephyrs to carry the noxious fumes far away, but the hotness of the day offered no deals or bargains.

As night fell, she carried on watching the flow of diggers as they tramped down the sides of the pit, then they plodded back up with armfuls of rock, soil and brick. Some now had hands missing. Beating bare fingers into rock and soil would soon do that to an unprotected human hand, numbed to pain and the constant chafe of aggressive rocks. Harsh friction against the derma would soon tear away the thin veneer that makes us human and not just a hunk of articulate, thinking and bleeding meat.

Lucy watched as they went down and came back up like dutiful worker ants.

What she didn't notice however was that less came up than went down.

She thought about Daryl Teever, the boy she'd being caught with in the cupboard. He'd never shown any interest in her before, nor she him. But that day at school, she felt a burning itch within herself that just had to be scratched there and then. The most she knew about the finer mechanics of sex was what she'd seen on TV, and things her friends had confessed. She'd never really seen a boy's *thing* before. Her father's peeking from behind a towel when she walked into the bathroom by mistake didn't count.

The urge had been an uncontrollable rush of vibrant emotion; Daryl Teever happened to be nearby and merely followed her lead. He was just a teenage boy; why wouldn't he say no. The rest had been on her. It was something that just needed to be done. She needed to be done. Even as she was taking off her school clothes during afternoon break, her thoughts never swayed from what she was doing or who she was with. Just a wanton urge that overtook her at that moment in time, regardless of the fact, she had English with the gorgeous Mr Brady last thing. One minute she was walking down the corridor to her lesson, next thing she realised, she was in the stationery cupboard door opening and the strangely hilarious, open mouth look on Mr Moor's face with his eyes focused on the position of her hand on Daryl's crotch.

Daryl had started to cry as Mr Moor led him away, while she pulled her clothes on in a hurry. Her tears, her shame, the letter; the rest was dire history.

The sun was close to finishing its warming of the day when her father's head appeared from the attic hole. Earnest and solemn, he said quietly, 'Lucy, would you come down stairs please, your mother wants to talk to you.'

'I'm not interested,' she answered from her perch of guilt, not taking her gaze from off the mesmerizing pit.

'All the same, we'd still like you to come down stairs.'

'They've started a fire,' Lucy replied, steering the conversation away from her.

'We've seen, we noticed when we woke up.'

'What do you think they're doing down there?'

'I dread to think.'

'We're watching them now. They're watching us watch them. He's watching us watch them watch us.'

'Who?'

Lucy pulled the binoculars away from her eyes and looked down upon her father, 'the man from my dream, I'm guessing.'

A chill shiver flowed down her father's spine, she visibly saw it happen. He rolled his shoulders to escape the spasm.

'I'll come down now.' She managed a weak smile then climbed down off the roof and through the attic, following her father downstairs to where her already tearful mother waited.

'Your mother and I have been talking,' her father announced as she entered the living room. He stood; her mother remained on the sofa, arms wrapped around herself, her face raw with tears.

'Yeah, and . . . ?'

Her mother let go a bout of tears.

'We were thinking about letting them have you.'

'What, who?'

'The Starers. It's clearly you that they want.'

'Them! You're gonna shove me outside?'

'It seems a possibility.' The words didn't seem to be coming from her father's mouth. It was more like he was mouthing the words and somebody else was talking in time with the movement of his lips. But she was wrong. He was saying these things.

'You're mad, the two of you.'

'It may be our only option.'

'You're being selfish. Why would you even think that? You're my parents; you're supposed to protect me!' Lucy pleaded.

'Just think about it. We don't even know what they want with you.'

'I'm guessing it's something to do with that mighty hole they've dug out for me. They want to bury me. Maybe I'm a sacrifice.'

A moment of silence reigned whilst everybody contemplated what to say. Kirsty spoke.

'It's going to be all three of us that go. Or just you, Lucy.'

'You can't make me go.'

'We won't force you to go. It'll have to be a sacrifice that you make,' Dylan offered.

'Are you being serious?'

'Are you sorry?' Kirsty asked her daughter. Tears had formed in both of their eyes now, quivering puddles that threatened to spill diamond drips down their red cheeks.

'Of course I'm sorry Mum! I'm sorry I lose my temper sometimes. I see this red mist and then before I know it, I've done something stupid. I can't help it! I need help, I'll see a doctor, just please don't give me up!'

Lucy tottered towards her mother and fell into her arms. They squeezed each other tight, all now crying. Dylan joined his wife and daughter, wrapping his arms around both of their necks.

'Lucy?' Dylan said.

'Yeah,' she sniffled.

'We're joking.'

'What?'

'We wouldn't really send you out there,' Kirsty confirmed, wiping a tear away with her sleeve.

'You were joking?'

Her parents both nodded.

'I should call you bastards.'

'No. No you shouldn't,' her mother warned in a playful manner as she stroked her hair.

'We just wanted you to realise that you can't carry on the way you have,' Dylan reasoned, 'these deranged outbursts will split this family apart if you keep going on the way you have. You've got to be grown up about things. We've got to work as a team.'

'I know Dad.'

'You need to promise to calm down and not be so . . . damned explosive all the time. There's no need!'

'I know.'

'Will you make an effort to change?'

'Yes, Dad.'

They all looked into each other's eyes. A team. Dylan felt a new sense of bonding between them. His heart glowed with joy, filling up and pouring out into a smile.

'Good, if we're going to get through this at all, we're going to get through this together.'

Kirsty and Lucy nodded, sinking heads into one another, bumping noggins, the trio, the family.

'Dad?'

'Yes, sweetie?'

'I want to go outside. Let's try it. I want to see what they'll do.'

'But . . .'

'I'm tired of waiting. Let's do or die. Let's see what happens.'

'You're very brave, darling. I was joking, but it's your choice.'

'I don't care. I just want to know what they want.'

'Kirsty?' Dylan asked.

'We'll be right behind you sweetie.'

'You won't push me out?' Lucy asked.

'We'll be holding your hand.'

'Okay, we do it now. While I'm psyched up.'

They moved as one to the hallway. Dylan removed the screws that fixed the door shut and secure. He popped them all on top of the little set of drawers beside the front door that they used as a dumping ground for keys, old receipts and junk mail. He opened the door with a creak and the stench of the filthy congregation hit them akin to a swarm of vile insects. Kirsty gagged with disgust, Dylan narrowed his eyes to the stinging vapours. Lucy however, steadied herself, bravely readying herself to face the audience that had gathered to meet her. She felt like she should smile as she greeted her 'fans'.

Another odour wafted on the breeze, a rotten egg smell that crinkled noses and tested their gag reflexes.

The sea of faces stared straight into her, unfaltering, devoid of any sense of emotion except apathy. She didn't dare take her eyes off them, even though her father held the edge of the door, ready to slam it shut at any sign of sudden movement. She still expected them to surge forward and rip the skin from her thin bones.

They didn't.
They just stared.
And stared.
And *stared.*

The silence reigned for a disquieting minute, each tribe staring each other out, but the only blinks came from the Keenes' eyes. The more they listened the more their ears became attuned to an underlying sound. Dylan recognised it as the Rice Krispy crackle from his dream and immediately remembered where he'd heard it before. Whilst delivering flat screen monitors to a power station, he'd passed under some thick, high voltage cables; the sound that the crowd emitted and the electrical fizz from the pylons were unmistakably the same.

Lucy searched behind for her parents' hands; they gripped her fingers, holding on tight. Lucy swallowed before addressing the crowd, as she thought it was the next natural step.

'What do you want?'

The electric silence hummed, the Keenes' quiet, concerned breaths the only sound to dislodge the stillness.

'Well?' she said, a little louder, more confident this time, 'tell me or go home. We're sick and tired of you, if you're not going to tell us, we're going to start getting angry.'

The blood-stained little girl blinked once as if she'd been chosen to receive the single message. Her marigold dressing gown (which now as they looked closer, they could see had patterns of waddling ducks and ducklings on it) was now camouflaged with a crust of Lennon's dark blood. They could just make out Lennon's trainers. The standing crowd covered the rest of him with trampling feet.

Lucy felt the hands holding her fingers tighten. Nobody said anything; to disturb the anticipation would soil whatever happened next.

The should-be-cute but now sinister-as-hell little girl spoke, in a voice that was sweet, yet somehow completely defied the situation and what they had expected from her. It was her voice, sounding from somewhere else; a recorded echo.

'He's not ready yet, not long now. He'll be here soon. He says be patient, Lucy. *Soon.*'

It was Kirsty who slammed the door, fingers lost and fumbling as they struggled with the key. It was Dylan that screamed. Lucy was the one to faint back into her parents' arms in a floppy child-like bundle.

Her head knocked back, drowsily giving up on reality, her heart beating out a scared arrhythmia.

Save me. Save me. Save me.

Somebody wanted her.

The man from her dreams

But not the man of *her* dreams.

Outside, electric eyes flickered on and off, a high speed cosmos until the crowd resembled a collection a deep sea creatures, strange, and rarely seen by the gaze of man. And for good reason.

At Home With The Keenes

How soon is now?
How soon is soon?
An Hour?
A Day?
A Minute?
A Blink?

Kirsty Keene's mind raced like the intricacies of a jet engine, the cryptic clue as to why they were here, only heeded more questions.

Soon . . .

They had pulled Lucy in by her shoulders and rested her on the sofa. Her body remained limp and floppy, useless muscles offered no fight against the gravity of the situation. They checked her eyes, which rolled lazily to the back of her head, with a torch they saw that they still dilated. She'd just fainted. The shock of the knowledge had knocked her for six that was all.

'Who is *he*?' Kirsty asked. A sickening ball of bile grew like a cancer in her stomach, as she feared the truth would be too much for her mind to digest.

'I don't know. I don't care. He's not having our daughter. I'll make sure of that.'

'How?'

'We go for the car. We go now. We take Lucy and we just drive. We plough through the fucking crowd. I don't care how many I kill.'

'They're still people Dylan!'

'They're in my way, now they can damn well get the fuck out of it!' Dylan angered. 'I'm not giving them a choice.'

'Okay,' Kirsty agreed, 'how do we get to the car? You saw what happened to Lennon.'

'We kill as many as we can before we even go outside. Lennon tried to go one on a hundred. We need to even the odds a little. Spread them out.'

'How?'

'Fire.'

'Where will we go?'

'North, I'm guessing everybody walked down to see us. We'll get so far north it'll take them a week to catch up with us.' Dylan stroked his daughter's head, sweeping away the thin strands of hair that had become glued to her forehead with sweat.

'Then what, just keep driving?'

'Anywhere's better than here.'

'You mean home?'

'It's more like a prison.'

Kirsty kept quiet. Silently she agreed with her husband, but at the back of her mind, the worst scenario played out. A man was coming for their daughter and he was going to take her away from them and do unimaginable things to her. This was a parent's worst fear, yet it was what was about to happen to them, unless they did something about it.

But what?

Kirsty didn't want to see the man, nor did she want to see what he planned on doing to her daughter. She wanted it all to end long before that.

Dylan stood up. He walked through to the kitchen, reluctant to leave his daughter. Kirsty relented and followed him through the utility and into the garage. He was filling a cardboard box with aerosol tins.

'What are you doing?'

'Having a bonfire. If you want to help, get some bottles of water and some food, bag it up and leave it by the front door. We need to travel light,' Dylan said as he dropped a bottle of turpentine into the cardboard box.

'You want to do this now?'

'*He* is coming!' he answered, transcending the voice of the little girl, '*soon*, you heard her. Only drunks and children tell the truth,' he laughed to himself, dropping a roll of duct tape into the box.

'So you're just going to burn them?'

'Yeah, thin them out a bit. Give us a bit more of a fighting chance.'

'I don't like it Dylan, all this death.'

'It's theirs or ours, pick a side darling. I'd rather live and fight than rollover and die.'

'I don't want to see any more death. Not ever.'

'We haven't a choice.'

'We do.' She had an idea in mind. A grim one.

'Well if it involves a way of getting out of here, I'm all ears.' He paused from filling up the box with flammable materials, turned and looked at her for an answer. Kirsty remained quiet and passive; with a bite of her bottom lip, she aimed her gaze outside. Avoiding his.

'I want good ideas. You're part of the solution or you're staying behind. I'm taking Lucy with me and I'm getting in that car. I have to protect her from *him*. I haven't got time to convince you to stay or go. You'll have to make up your own mind. Don't make me drag you out.'

Kirsty kept quiet. Dylan stood up with the box clasped to his chest and left the garage. He stopped in the utility and looked out the back door. A grey laugh opened up across his thinning cheeks. Kirsty joined him and followed his gaze.

As expected, Mrs Loughery was standing in the garden, her cheeks had sunk inwards from a few days of malnutrition, her once finely coiffured hair resembled an eagle's nest, a pigeon sat upon her head, scratching round in the dark strands and making itself comfortable. A thick line of vile, off-white had been splattered down over her shoulder and across her sumptuous breasts. She remained unflinching even though the bird had taken a hefty dump on her.

Dylan laughed and pointed at her, then looked at Kirsty.

'That's why I want to get out of here. Look! They belong here now, they're part of the damned furniture; even the birds agree for Christ sake!' Dylan left his wife and bounded upstairs. Lucy was still unconscious on the sofa; he left her there safe for the time being. Kirsty meanwhile went to the medicine cabinet in the utility room.

Dropping his box of wares on the landing, Dylan headed up into the loft; taking the binoculars with him, he climbed onto his vantage point atop the ridge and spied on what was happening around the pit.

Smoke.

Flames.

Not from the crashed plane, but from something else. It was a fresh burn from beneath.

But nobody was moving rock and soil. The industry on the former playing field had ground to an unnerving halt.

The crowd stood around the formed crater looking in the direction of the house. Well, Lucy to be exact.

Whatever they were digging out, they had dug out. It no longer required their unique attention. Many of the group circling the pit had hands missing, some had bony stumps. Others still had hands attached, albeit missing skin was held together by thin strands of tendons and torn flesh.

They resembled famine victims, emancipated, white skulls fighting out from the skin on their faces; a holocaust convention at Madame Tussauds. They were finished, their end was nigh. Dylan could feel it. Physically they couldn't last much longer without food or water. Their brains were obviously dead, it was a matter of time before their bodies gave up.

Unless *he* got to them first.

As if the hive before him was reading his mind, they began to move. From the edges of the pit, they started to part, creating a human corridor. The opening of people stepping to one side gathered direction, the expanse leading towards the house. Towards Lucy.

He was coming.

Soon.

No. *Now.*

Every muscle melted to a thin, useless jelly. Kneecaps and elbows suddenly became greasy hinges. Dylan's hand started to quake. He dropped the binoculars, his shaking, palsied fingers reached out uselessly as the lenses skittered off the roof. An air bubble formed in his head as he felt like fainting from the shock. Dylan lurched forward, lost his balance, tumbled and fell.

If this was his final moment on this earth, his last poetic words would have been,

'*Oh fuck!*'

The Second Movement

By a cruel twisting sense of luck, of which he thought he didn't deserve, Dylan Keene didn't plummet to his doom and die at that moment. Fate had other plans in store for him, letting the feeling come back to his fingers as he rolled down the roof, enabling him to grasp onto the hole he had made through the tiles. He felt a jarring scrape. The friction from the slide broke off two fingernails from his left hand from which spurted thick, dark, blood. Tense, white fingers, slick with hot blood gripped on for dear life on the top edge of the tile around the bottom of the hole, whilst his legs dangled over the edge of the gutter, feet waving at the dumb crowd below.

A plastic smack from below confirmed the notion that he'd hit one of the unfortunates below with the dropped binoculars.

He didn't turn to look; instead he edged his knee up and wriggled back onto the roof. Once clinging safely to the roof hole, he breathed a sigh of welcome relief then looked at the ends of his fingers, shaking the accumulated blood from the tips. He winced. Deep red droplets rained down, soaking into the lichen decorated, rough grain of the tiles. The tips of his fingers throbbed and pulsated as blood was fed out into the air. The nail on his middle finger was missing, whilst a jagged half remained triumphantly on his ring finger, proud, though gory.

Whilst Dylan had being preoccupied with his wound, the crowd before him, the mass that had gathered outside his front door was splitting like a cell, dividing to become two parts. Everybody edged out of the way to construct a corridor lined by people.

Dylan adjusted his gaze and squinted. Through the swirling mists of smoke and redness of the fire came a figure highlighted against the backdrop. The injured fingertips were forgotten, the pain lost to a vision.

It was real.

He was real.

The stranger was coming towards the house.

He was coming towards the house.

Soon he would be here.

Maybe a hundred metres away, walking slowly.

He . . .

Soon . . .
'Oh fuck . . .'

BEHIND EVERY GOOD MAN..

.

Scramble would have been a good word to describe the way in which Dylan moved from the roof onto the landing, moving so fast he came close to adding another injury to his numerous faults, nearly breaking a leg as he jumped/fell from the attic on to the landing.

He picked up his box of tricks and moved to the landing window overlooking the crowd, swinging it wide open to face his attentive audience.

Taking a can of fly spray and a strip of torn off duct tape, Dylan taped the button down, and tossed the quickly emptying can into the crowd, not too close to the car. He repeated this with some peach air freshener, oven cleaner and a tin of deodorant.

Christ, if I had more time I could clear a few more.

He tossed the contents of the box outside into the centre of the front garden crowd, keeping behind the bottle of turpentine and a thin rip of cardboard he had torn from the box. Again, the shaking fingers came back as he twisted the top off the turpentine.

He watched as across the road, the old man who had waited and watched in the rain so diligently stepped out from behind the stalled bus full of stinking passengers. The corridor of people was getting closer, creeping yet surging like a stalking predator. The Stranger from the pit was also getting closer, half way across the field now. The figure was clearer now.

Dylan rammed the strip of cardboard into the open neck of eye wateringly fragrant turpentine.

Lennon had helpfully left his lighter on the windowsill, as if strangely before death, he knew this moment was coming, aiding the fight of the future.

Dylan struck up the Zippo and held it to the cardboard wick, the flame munching upwards as it took hold. He watched for a second ensuring it was sufficiently lit, then tossed it into the centre of the garden crowd, down to where the hissing aerosol canisters lay in wait.

The explosion was instantaneous, a bright, flushing bark of light then the flame spreading out beneath and atop the crowd as the turpentine spilt out. No one screamed. They just stood and burned. The first canister ignited a few seconds later, ignited the escaping aerosol, turning it into a rocket that shot off towards the garden wall. It ricocheted around the lawn crowd, igniting their clothes further. Moments later the other canisters ignited, causing similar mayhem as the high pressure containers ignited and zig-zagged amongst the crowd. The front garden was now ablaze, the hungry stench of burning flesh and hair offended Dylan's nostrils. He gagged and pulled the window shut, this time pocketing the lighter before heading downstairs, Lucy still in her prone faint shape upon the sofa. Dylan bent down and slapped her hard and sharp on the cheek. She jarred awake and alert with wide-eyed shock.

'Kirsty!' he shouted through to the kitchen, 'we're going!'

He got no answer. A sublet hint of sickly sweetness hit his nose, replacing the stinking human inferno outside.

'What's wrong . . .' Lucy said as she stirred back to consciousness. Then as she saw the fiery wall in the front garden, 'Jesus Christ, Dad! What did you do?'

'He's coming, we're going. Now!'

Lucy jumped up alert and frightened, for once listening to her father in the first instant.

As Dylan grabbed one of the makeshift spears from the kitchen table, he found why his wife didn't answer him.

The empty packets of various painkillers, sleeping pills, aspirin and paracetamol alongside the finished off bottle of rum, lead him to the obvious conclusion that she'd taken an overdose. Kirsty was slumped in the corner of the kitchen; a line of dark dribble escaped her mouth, seeping like syrup from her twisted head.

A slow rise in her chest showed that she was still breathing.

'Shit, shit, shit, shit . . . oh shit, Kirst, why, why?' Dylan knelt down next to her, he slapped her cheek as he had Lucy's. She wasn't coming round anytime soon.

This was her escape.

Death.

The Bitch. The stupid selfish Bitch. Not now, please not now, not the Baby!

Anything to shelter her eyes from witnessing whatever that monster had planned for his daughter. Death. Sweet, selfish death.

'You don't get away that easily Kirsty,' Dylan said, lifting his wife's head to face his. Taking his middle and index fingers, he shoved them as far as he could down into her throat. This was his first thought in effort to purge the poisons that were infiltrating his wife's body.

It felt warm and wet, strangely pleasant, her teeth scraped his fingers as her gag reflex kicked in, then a tide of sweet brown liquid spurted out from her mouth, little half dissolved pills clinging to the sweet rum like flotsam.

'What's happened to Mum? What have you done?' Lucy asked from behind.

'She's poorly, get her some water,' he said an instant before sticking his fingers in again to remove any further poison from her system. Kirsty vomited again, projecting further this time, splattering Dylan's chest.

'That's better darling, get it all out.' Dylan patted his wife between the shoulder blades

He turned to Lucy, 'get some water in her. I'm off to warm up the car and have a word with the neighbours.'

Lucy nodded, strange emotions shredding through her discombobulated nervous system. She grabbed a bottle of water and tended to her rousing mother.

Dylan picked up a makeshift spear constructed from a bread knife and a mop handle then headed to the front door with dire purpose.

HE . . .

As he had hoped, the fire had thinned the crowd. Some had collapsed after their musculature had burnt away, failing to support their weakening weight any further against gravity and the hungry gnawing of the fire.

Knowing what had to be done to get where he wanted to be, Dylan let the red mist wash over him, a warm, welcoming tide to bask in his murderous rage.

No more Mister Nice Guy, as the saying goes.

The red mist thickened, becoming an impenetrable ink that clouded his vision. *Is this a prelude to violence?* He asked himself. *Is this what the mind does; draws a curtain to shade the mind from the horrors it allows the body to commit?* That's what murderers say in court in their defence; *I don't remember. I don't remember doing it. I don't remember a thing. . .*

The curtain was fixed, inhibiting Dylan the sight to see through his own mind. The strain of the situation, a want to avenge his brother's death, the abject fear for his family's wellbeing all added up and multiplied against each other, equalling this state of mind where he now found himself.

Dylan Keene lost it, not caring whether or not he ever got it back.

He stabbed without remorse, or conscience, or guilt, holding onto a sense of grim determination of right over wrong, or a wrong over an even greater wrong; the possible demise of his family. It took less than thirty seconds, armed with only the spear (to distance himself from the Starers bizarre, electric, exploding touch) to pierce the hearts of the bloodstained little girl, (whose voice had been used to transmit that sinister message from *he, who was yet to be named),* the remaining paramedic and about ten of his fire blackened neighbours that had besieged his family.

I am not a murderer.

All is fair in love and war.

He closed his eyes tight before each impact, trying his best to lessen the burn upon his memory. The less he remembered about this day, the better. He wasn't a monster. He took no pleasure in this.

He was a father, a husband, and a brother.

Not a murderer.

All is fair in love and war.

They had all died quietly and with as less suffering as possible. None screamed as he punctured the remaining life from their earthly vessels, none looked as he stole their pitiful lives from them. It had needed to be done; given the situation, he could see no other option in order to save his family. He had as little choice in it as they did. All he had to do was get in the car and go, but the fear still remained of the Starers suddenly advancing forward and descending upon him.

The fire had died down now. Having burnt up its brief spell of energy, it now smouldered on the burnt out lawn and the clothes of his brain dead enemies. Those still standing still stared at the house behind him. At Lucy.

It's not murder. It's not murder. It's not. It's not. It's not.

All is fair in love and war.

This is survival.

When Dylan emerged from his murderous trance, he had a path to the car as well as dozens of bleeding and burnt bodies at his feet, not all of his own doing.

He looked down; Lennon's hand, black from fire and swollen fat and sausage-like with decomposition, lay gripped in a loose fist at his feet. The plastic car keys partially melted, the ring still hanging off a charred little finger. Dylan bent low, and with a little force, he managed to pry the key ring out from of his dead brother's death grip. Nearby he spied Lennon's now infamous De-Brainer Bat, which had rolled as far as it could before it rested on the rusty bloodied screw.

When Dylan looked up, the remaining crowd shuffled forward as one. Across the road in between the walls of the people corridor, walked the Stranger. He was staring at Dylan with a confident, hypnotising smile, no rush ushered his walk. He strolled with a casual arrogance. He passed the back of the bus and towards the ambulance on Dylan's side of the road. He was what, twenty metres away? Maybe thirty seconds left before striking distance, ambling casually toward the house, without a care in world.

Except for his daughter and whatever devious ways he intended to spend with her.

The Stranger's eyes bore into Dylan, and for the briefest of moments, an invading movie played in his mind's eye, it only lasted a second, but the flash told Dylan everything he needed to know.

A passenger jet, a chorus of people screaming; the stranger has a knife in his hand; he's encouraging another man to stab a stewardess. His voice is calm as he rests a hand on the young man's shoulder. Out of one of the windows, Dylan makes out a cityscape, only a few hundred metres below, the engines roar with the fighting strain against gravity. People scream. The stranger smiles as the plane tilts. . .

Celeste Marks took a step forward, the once loved face from Dylan's past. Except now that face was blackened with smoky soot, her bra had burnt off revealing a red raw skinned breast, her once lustrous auburn hair had singed off on one side of her still steaming scalp, giving her the appearance of a tortured Barbie Doll. It was safe to say that her looks had vastly deteriorated over the devastating last few minutes.

Call it bittersweet revenge Celly, for breaking my heart, no hard feelings, yeah?

Still reeling from the stranger's vision, Dylan shook the invading image from his mind, levelled the spear and launched it at his ex, half serving as futile warning to the others, half a bitter revenge for screwing his life up so damned well. He cared about the family he had left, not her. She'd had her chance and screwed it up. She was as a good a target as any. She didn't matter much anymore. Just another face in the crowd, they all were faces in the same crowd.

Dylan Keene struck out against his past.

The blade caught her in the lower neck, severing an artery. The bread knife spear fell away and tumbled to her feet. She didn't drop, instead she stood, stared and bled, the dark blood washing out over her soot stained skin, a grim waterfall. . .

Another vision penetrated his mind as if it was one of his own memories.

Dylan looks upon a room; two men are by a window looking down onto a city street. One is the stranger; the other is a young man with a rifle. The stranger is talking in a low, hushed, delicate tone, soothing even; yet his voice raises to say "NOW!" as a Lincoln Continental drives past on the street below. The first shot misses its target. The second however, catches a man sitting on the rear seat in the neck, while the third impacts with the back of his head. The stranger pats the young man on the shoulder, nodding and smiling. Nodding and smiling . . .

'Lucy get out here now!' Dylan called, blinking away the second vision. He didn't turn. He kept his eyes on the crowd shuffling forward, the bubbling crimson geyser that erupted from his ex, and *him*.

Another vision, an unwanted gift from the stranger . . .

Everybody is wearing clothes from a different era, maybe twenties or early thirties. A party in full swing, the smell of spilt alcohol and cigar smoke taint the air. The stranger sits in the corner whispering into the ear of a sober young man with a funny moustache on his top lip. Dylan thinks he looks like a more severe Charlie Chaplin. It's not Charlie Chaplin at all, but it could be. Everybody is speaking in loud, gregarious German. The stranger hands the young man a book, pointing to it and giving him a firm pat on the shoulder. Nodding and smiling, nodding and smiling. . .

Lucy joined her father at his side. Her jaw jutted out as she clenched her teeth in abject fear. Her eyes were wide, darting back and forth, as she drank in the situation around them.

'Your mother?' he asked quickly.

'She wouldn't get up. I gave her some water, she won't wake . . . is . . . that . . . him?' Lucy pointed at the approaching stranger with a gently quaking finger.

'It would appear so.'

'What are we gonna do? Are we leaving Mum?'

'I don't want to . . . but we don't have much choice . . . or time. Dammit!' Dylan readied the De-Brainer bat, wishing he hadn't thrown the spear at Celeste after all.

It's hot. The sun burns bright and white upon a hill above a desertscape. A gathered crowd dressed in robes jeer and holler in a language Dylan can't even begin to comprehend. Stones are thrown at a bloodied, naked man fixed to a crucifix. He raises his head and looks down upon the stranger, shaking his head weakly. The stranger smiles, pleasant and satisfied.

The stranger stepped closer; they could both see who he was, though neither recognized him; he looked like any ordinary human male, tall, handsome, clean shaven; a successful salesman or a male model perhaps. Healthy tanned skin, slightly Middle Eastern looks; however there was a hint of European about him, like a roguish gypsy or a deceitful spy. Dylan didn't know for sure, but the Stranger had come from beneath the ground after a long wait. What he also didn't know was that he'd had every grain of the clinging soil licked clean from his skin by the devoted Starers.

He carried with him the rotting egg reek of sulphur, an all-encompassing stench that turned their stomachs over in a bilious wave. Their inside natures warned them of his this odour, their bodies fearing the touch of its vapour.

He could be any woman's dream man, yet Dylan got the divine impression that he could take any form. In this case, he had taken the guise of a gentleman. His daughter would find him alluring. Just to make it easier when he did whatever he planned to do to her. He looked so damned normal and that was the scary thing. He could be anybody. Yet something else set him apart from the crowd even further than his looks.

His clothes; what he wore disturbed them both, striking them dumb where they stood. . .

He wore a coat of human faces, grisly stitched and held together with thick woven strands of human hair, covering him as any macabre shroud should, bent and empty noses stuck up from the shoulders, maybe thirty or so faces, some only halves where the perfect tear had failed, he had stitched them on, regardless of their condition. Some eyelids had been sewn shut; others gaped like toothless second and third mouths. Patches of bloody, sticky hair adorned it in places. Some had beards. Clearly, he wanted to make a horrifying first impression. By the time they had taken in the appalling sight, *He* was standing in the driveway. *He* was here. *Soon* was gone. His shadow was lost amongst the crowds, for his was missing, he scattered light differently somehow, defied it.

He without a shadow spoke in a voice that was both young and old.

'I only want her,' he said with a pleasant and winning smile that made you want to put all your trust and savings into his care. His tone was convincing, like that of a friend you'd loan your car to, knowing that you'd get it back in one piece.

'If you put up a fight, it won't be pretty. I'll take you apart atom by atom. Leave me be and I'll let you and whatever is left of your wife alone. I won't trouble you again. I promise.' The stranger vainly put his hand to his chest, as if the simple gesture acted as guarantee for his word. 'Give her to me, I just want the girl,' he repeated.

Dylan remained stoic, he didn't want to start a war of words with this fella, don't enter into any agreements, offer no handshake, voice no opinion, because somehow, he'll twist it and come back to haunt him one day. Maybe even today.

Over my dead body, Dylan thought as he ground his teeth to potential dust.

'That can be arranged my friend, quite easily,' the stranger said in a sparse instant.

Now he knew that the stranger had a foothold in his mind. He suddenly became aware of invisible fingers massaging unused portions of his grey matter. It was soothing, almost hypnotic and intoxicating. He shook his head and looked to his scared daughter.

Dylan handed the car keys to Lucy then toyed with the De-Brainer, slapping the fat end into his hand. Say nothing. *Give him nothing.*

'I'm not who you think I am. I'm a mirage, an apparition at most. I'm not *him*. Nobody is; but we all are in our own little ways.'

Dylan cocked his head at the comment. The Stranger held his palms up to the sky as if holding up an invisible beam, then turned his hands and levelled them by his side. It started to rain thick, leaden drips from a clear sky.

'So be it; your dead body it is. I tried to make it easy for you,' the grim coated stranger stepped forward with purpose and that forever lasting smile. His skin coat flapped open, revealing his taut and toned nakedness beneath. Dylan shivered sickly, his mind's cinema imagining the stranger's gruesome designs on his daughter. To even up with the rain, the sky began to darken as the thick droplets descended with intensity. Clouds of black tumbled into the blue, forming from nowhere, colouring in a slate coloured sky.

'I'm sure I can get your wife involved with my plans, I know what she *really* likes.'

Dylan got ready to raise the rain-slickened bat, standing in front of Lucy, using every ounce and seconds left of his life to protect her. It's what good parents did since time began. Protect the young at all costs, even if it cost you an eye or worse.

The stranger was fast. He became a blur. Reaching up, he grabbed the wet bat from Dylan's grasp, minute splinters catching his already bleeding fingers as it was rasped from his hands. The Stranger threw it against the Loughery's house wall, where it bounced then rolled as far as it could down the drive.

A low left punch shattered two of Dylan's ribs as if they were made of brittle bone china. A rapid right uppercut cracked his jawbone turning it into an enamel vice, slamming tooth against tooth, knocking out three teeth, one of which he swallowed with a slick shot of sharp salty blood. He spat out the others from his grisly mouth with a choking gurgle; they rolled down the slope of the driveway like dice in a game of the macabre.

He fell back hard on the block paving, cracking an elbow that sent a sickening feeling down into his empty pit of a stomach. The unnatural rain drenched his back, causing his clothes to cling and weigh down his movements as if he'd been washed down with liquid lead. He wanted to throw up, but at the same time, a strong desire to breathe overcame him as he dragged in a wheezing lungful of tightened, foul oxygen. The stench of burnt death, Kirsty's vomit on his clothes, the reek of human foulness and his own impending doom made it a thousand times worse than he ever expected. Was this death? Is this how the last grim last moment kicks off?

Dylan looked at his own blood splattering thick, bright and real, congealing on the driveway, his code, his DNA. A strange though lucid thought process occurred to him as he looked upon his own escaping blood, a sharpened clarity that defined the situation. Was that why he, Lennon and Kirsty had been spared? They all had genes relating to Lucy, whatever spell had been cast across the crowd, turning them into meaty statues, somehow didn't apply to them. He only wanted her, and this was his way of keeping her in one place whilst he was roused from the belly of the earth. He, his brother and his wife had only been spared from being hypnotised because of some magical genetic loophole. It was only a theory, but it made him feel better that he had some understanding of the situation that had unfolded outside of 68 Westfield Road. It was family that held them together, nothing could tear that apart. Not distance, nor evil, nor fall out over trivial matters. Family fought together.

The Stranger stood over him, a mocking smile plastered across his cheeks. His coat of un-staring faces breezed open, exposing his nakedness beneath. The organ that dangled before Dylan's eyes didn't belong on any human; it was more animal or creature even; out of proportion, a caricature of a monster's phallus. Dylan reasoned that the stranger had every intention of putting that *thing* inside his daughter. He wouldn't be surprised if it had a set of smiling teeth.

The Stranger grabbed the dumbfounded Lucy, throwing her on the rain speckled bonnet with a tinny thump, and began to pull off her jogging bottoms with eager, inquisitive fingers. He tossed them over Dylan's head where they landed behind him. Lucy screamed as the Stranger held her down, gripping her throat with thickset hands that looked like they could snap her trachea with no more than a flick of his fingers.

Dylan felt the vomit rise. He felt weak and useless; he was blinded by the pain in his jaw and had all but given up. The pelting rain hammered his thoughts, drumming a distracting tattoo that soothed and warned his mind away from the unfolding matters.

The Stranger opened his grim coat; a live tentacle slithered out appearing to sniff and taste the air. A syrupy, clear yellow liquid dripped from the end of the monstrous proboscis as it extended forward with eager glee. With his free hand, he began to thumb Lucy's heart patterned girl boxers to one side; Dylan would never forget the wanton and ill smile on the Stranger's face for as long as he lived. It was a haunting grin that belonged on the face of madness.

Again, Lucy screamed; a beseeching, primeval shriek that cut through the air and into his soul, causing him to shudder. She screamed again and again; every breath was recycled into an urgent, shiver-inducing vocal.

Do something.

Dylan felt paralysed by fear or maybe even the Stranger's evilly divine influence. With no hope in sight, all he could do was lay uselessly on the floor like a paraplegic slug, the rain drenching him further. He turned his head, to one side he could see Lucy's jogging pants, beneath them lay the De-Brainer.

Dylan willed for his hand to move. He found it a struggle to draw breath from the sheer terror he felt pressing down on him. This monster was going to impregnate his daughter with something he didn't even want to contemplate. This is what it was all about; fucking, a simple action which kept the world turning and fighting. It's what all life was about when you got down to it. Rutting and impregnating to keep the population topped up. That's why it was so easy. That's why death was so easy too, an effort by nature to counteract our fornications.

Dylan's gaze switched from his daughter's outreaching fingers to the terrified expression on her face. She screamed again as the heathen's tentacle stroked its wet end against her bare thigh, leaving a sticky trail of rancid goo. The white flesh began to steam and sizzle; the Stranger's seed was caustic. Why wouldn't it be?

Dylan retreated within himself, imagining a world without Kirsty's home cooked meals, without his daughter's scathing though witty comments; without Lennon's daft banter . . . scratch the last one. Lennon was gone. It was this bastard's fault. The hate intensified, burning a red flare in his soul, lighting him up. Dylan wanted to ram the De-Brainer up the fucker's arse and rag it about twisting his insides to mush. He wanted to cram his thumbs deep into his eye sockets and tickle his brain with his nails before pulling his face apart like an orange. He wanted to break his fingers off one by one and force-feed them down his vile throat, then start on his toes. That appendage wanted chopping off and flushing down the toilet. He wanted . . . Dylan's fingers twitched, his palm flexed.

The red mist descended through the fugue, then inked a pure and hateful black.

Hate made him want to love. The thought of his loves taken away forced him into action. This was a power more potent than the Stranger's influence, which when you realised, the power of evil was nothing more than a tangible thing, something that given the strength of will, could be broken as easily as glass. Nothing could take the place of a strong and willing human heart, not when action needed to be done, for the just of good.

Good was as strong as evil. Don't believe the lies that try and taint your heart.

Lucy gave a soundless scream as the Stranger moved into her. Her body buckled into a C-shape, banging the back of her head against the bonnet with a dull and violent thud. A clicking croak escaped her mouth as her fists pounded the agony out upon the metal mattress. The croak rose to a seething little girl scream as the Stranger began to slide his hips back and forth, back and forth. His grin was fixed in a grisly pleasure.

The only thought in Lucy Keene's reeling mind wasn't of her dead uncle or her disabled father, or the fact her mother had tried to kill herself only minutes ago.

It was the ache. More than physical, it was like someone had stuck a hot needle into her soul and punctured her very being. Today was a day of change; she would never be the same again. Nobody would.

She blacked it out, thinking that old adage that people wonder when they find themselves in horrible, unthinkable situations.

Think Happy Thoughts. Think Happy Thoughts. Think Happy Thoughts .
.

Breaking out from the paralysis, Dylan concentrated his growing reach and began to pull and tug on the leg of the jogging bottoms. They caught on the decking screw, dragging the bat along. He grabbed the bat by the handle and with his strength exploding, swung it round, imbedding the rusty screw into the back of the Stranger's ankle. They both let out a roar, one of sheer pain, one of delighted triumph.

The Stranger released his controlling grip of Lucy; the bizarre snake dripping with bright blood and sexual effluence slid out from between Lucy's legs as she pulled free from his grasp and rolled sideward over the bonnet. Dylan twisted up and pulled the De-Brainer out from the Stranger's Achilles heel. Thick, black blood seeped down his ankle and over his foot, hissing when it touched the driveway as it burnt away the life of clinging lichen and collected moss. The Stranger nearly fell down on his good leg before righting himself on the bonnet, trying to regain his stance.

'You're not going to let me finish all the way are you?' The Stranger asked with a raised theatrical eyebrow.

'Luce get in the car, we're going for a drive,' Dylan painfully called out to Lucy, pulling his eyes away from the thing that dangled like a fat, pink, eyeless snake. It righted itself, seemingly sniffing the air towards Lucy, hungry for her. She did as she was told, unlocking the car and climbing in, except she hopped across to the driver seat.

The Stranger turned to Lucy, teeth seething in a bitter grimace.

'It's me and you Lucy. We're going to change the world *together.* Everything's going to be different. We need to be a team for it to work though. I didn't choose you. You're just the one of many,' he reasoned, as if he believed he was right, his gospel was the only way.

The Stranger turned back to Dylan and smiled oily, 'you're going nowhere. You're going to die right here at this spot, it's going to hurt; then I'm taking all my brides of this earth, as I always have done, millennia after millennia. You can't stop me, not even when I'm in my earthly form. The brief fighting beat of the human heart isn't enough for my cunning.'

Dylan shuffled back against the wall of his house then shifted towards the Loughery's. He noticed that the crowd had stopped moving, they were giving *him* space. That was good. He shuffled again, maintaining his nervous posture. The Stranger took a step forward as well, as he continued his righteous speech.

'. . . why must you people fight. Every time I come to the surface in one form or another, you always demand on settling arguments with war. And yet, you always lose in the end . . .'

Dylan shifted further back. From the corner of his eye, he saw his daughter nod then smile, baring her teeth as fear fixed upon her face. He nodded back.

'. . . what you people call evil, always prevails in the end. Always. Good might last a while, but evil deeds scar longer and deeper. Far longer as you're about to find out my friend, death will outlive life. My ways are forever . . .'

A weak cough came from the front doorway, which briefly shifted the Stranger's attention away from Dylan. Kirsty's hand peeked out from the doorway, fingers pulling her along the blood stained front step. The Stranger turned back to face the car as Lucy turned the key. His face slack and blank as if to say. *What are you doing little girl?*

The Corsa engine choked, and then roared as the gears grinded. Dylan lifted his legs up and rolled backward over his aching shoulders as the car jumped forward. The front bumper punching with a tonne of metal violence into the Stranger's legs, pushing him down beneath the bumper, pinning the back of his knees to the front of the house with a pounding snap, drowned out by the tremendous growl of the engine and collision of metal unto brick and bone. It seemed that his earthly vessel that he carried himself in had the capacity for pain, the blood freezing scream testament to this fact.

He scowled and screamed at Lucy's betrayal, fists banging and hammering violently on the bonnet of the Corsa. His overly long nails scraped the paint off in eight desperate and jagged lines with a knife on ceramic shriek. He was trapped and he feared it. With the mere blink of his wide eyes, the crowd stepped forward, arms outstretched. While they carried out his orders, he failed to notice Dylan's rapid actions, who offered no remorse for this vile other worldly creature. Good was programmed to fight evil no matter what the odds. It was a genetic code that predispositions us to fight the good fight. Some men were cowards, but Dylan Keene did not possess that detrimental trait. He had a family. He had to be a hero for them, like all good fathers and husbands; he would fight for his family until the last drop of blood had been drained from his staggering being. All it took for evil to prevail was for good men to do nothing. All it takes for chaos to reign is for order to fail.

With teeth bared, Lucy revved the engine into the red. The tyres squealed as the car pushed harder and harder into the stranger and the wall. Acrid smoke poured out from the wheel arches. She held it well, the worry that she'd stall it hung over Dylan.

'Stay away from my family . . . you dirty . . . old . . . bastard!' Dylan spat, then swung out hard, aiming for the head this time, as Dylan was confident that no true heart existed within the confines of its dark chest, only a mockery of a muscle.

The already blood-stained screw impacted with the stranger's forehead, burrowing in to the hilt, knocking him back with a neck-snapping lurch. His skull opened up with a coconut cracking satisfaction. The Stranger ceased his screaming fit; a brief, gargling, choking sound escaped his throat, clicking away the final seconds of his life. Then he slumped forward, the bat still embedded firmly in his skull pointed towards three o'clock.

The crowd stopped their advance. All at once the unmanageable thousands surrounding the Keene household all collapsed limply in unison to the ground, their weakened bodies crumpling under their own weight. The soft thump that followed came as a sweetly toned resonance to their ears.

The roaring engine ceased, quieting down to a now steaming hiss and purr.

The crackle of the crowd ceased, the static hum cut off abrupt and definite, yet somehow Dylan's mind carried on the soundtrack, repeating a tinnitus loop.

The torrential rain stopped, the operatic rushing drum of the leaden raindrops left their senses as abruptly as they'd come into them.

A steel giant groaned from across the road. Dylan watched as the bus that had sat outside his house full of festering passengers for the last few days, set into motion and began to roll down the road, the driver now comatose and unaware. The 815 bus to Abcastle resumed its run that had become stalled by events beyond the control of the bus timetable, heading down Westfield road systematically crunching idle pedestrians beneath its unrelenting weight.

Lucy climbed out from the car and rushed around to be with her father, threw her arms around him and hugged him tight, hurting his broken ribs, but in a good way. The pain was good; it meant he was alive, breathing and kicking. He spat out a bright spit of blood.

'I love you, Dad, thank you.'

'I know you do. I'm glad you remembered your driving lessons on the airfield.' She held him tighter; lesson accomplished.

Over And Over And Over

The De-Brainer Bat fell off the steaming bonnet with a tinny thump. Dylan and Lucy watched as black oil flowed out from the stranger's eyes, mouth and the crevice in his forehead. Thick rivulets slimed over the bonnet, pushing stranded droplets of water from off the car.

The Stranger's head began to deflate as all liquid escaped the body, until it was a tanned sack of skin. The skin creased, then mottled like time-lapse footage of a diseased leaf. It broke apart before Dylan Keene's eyes. Flakes of skin floated gently away on the river of black, travelling like flotsam over rapids as they were carried away down the Corsa's front wing and onto the rain-dampened driveway.

Within a few more seconds, his entire body had deliquesced into an oily puddle beneath the car, seeping through the spaces in the block paving; all that physically remained of the stranger was the tattered coat of faces lying crumpled on the bonnet of the car.

The Stranger left their lives as he had come into it, grisly and weird, and with no mortal or earthly explanation.

It had ended. It was over.

A creak came from the front door, they both looked over. Kirsty Keene had crawled to the porch steps. Weak and drenched in perspiration, she was still alive. The impromptu stomach pump had saved her life and what was left of her sanity. She held a pale and shaking hand towards them, beckoning them over. Without hesitation, they rushed around the car avoiding the dark puddle that sizzled away the lichen, moss and anything unfortunate to be in its path, joining the matriarch of their family. Crouching down beside her, they cradled her weakened form in their arms.

'What happened?' her voice was as delicate as a fine petal, easily crushed by a bitter and cruel wind. They all embraced, wrapping arms around one another.

'It's over; fixed it, don't worry no more. We're safe.' He kissed her head, the sweat tasted fucking marvellous. The dead don't sweat. His babies were alive. He was alive. The surging sense of joy was like nothing he had felt before, a euphoric paroxysm of delight, better than any illicit drug, any joyous song or any pleasure for that matter. His family was alive. He was alive. They'd made it.

'I'm sorry Dylan . . . I . . .'

'Shhh, no more, you're weak, it's okay, just rest, we'll fix you up.'

Dylan looked down at the browning and blackened remains of his brother. He was nothing more than a voided and empty vessel now. A memory of a good man remains. Despite his impediments of character, Lennon had been an excellent brother, sticking with Dylan throughout their lives; they had rarely fought as children and had always remained firm friends. Dylan had the feeling that if he and Kirsty had another child, a boy, he already knew what he would name him.

Some of the crowd started to stir, drunkenly sitting up. They looked around bewildered with the situation; a few looked curiously towards the trio of Keenes for answers.

'We'll have to fix them all up.'

For this moment was theirs. They embraced, holding each other as much as their various pains would allow. Happiness reigned as the first sunset of many melted away the troubles of the black day. The fading warmth on their faces as the celestial bulb blast its final glowing of the day upon them.

The family Keene looked into each other's eyes and smiled. Kirsty's were half open, still drowsy from her attempted overdose, Dylan's were bound closed in contentment, dreaming of a new life, a better life, a move away, a new career, anything to break from the norm he had burrowed himself into.

Lucy's eyes were a beautiful baby blue.

She blinked; they were now an electric sea green.

Another blink. Then they were red.

This was her world, she wouldn't be a bride, but she could be something else. A leader the world hadn't seen before. This world was hers for the taking. The Stranger had known this; it was why she was one of a chosen few of the right mindset.

Then her eyes were brown, as they always would be.

One of the Starers close by sat up. His skin was charred and raw, his eyes black.

Dylan looked behind him as another sat up in the centre of the burnt front lawn, an elderly woman, another set of black eyes. Then another sat up, then another. All staring at Lucy.

Something slithered through the wet grass, something oily, black and ominous. It moved as a collection of mindful black droplets that had escaped through the cracks of the drive, splitting into individuals, slipping like black tears into the eyes and into the taken minds of the Starers. The ominous black oil should have trickled away into the caverns beneath the earth, to form and plan further atrocities; but instead it seemed, it still had business to attend to. This messenger from below wasn't done delivering his sermon just yet. Lessons had to learnt, a greater hell would be unleashed. Revenge was to be had.

One by one, they stood up over the trio. Celeste Marks stood up, bloody and black. More black-eyed Starers joined the standing crowd. More stood up and upon the broken and beaten Dylan, Kirsty and Lucy, they advanced.

One as many, many as one.

Lucy screamed. They all screamed.

It was far from over; in fact it wasn't even the beginning.

Dylan didn't fully understand this new evil, he hadn't the time. There wasn't time for questions, only action.

With a groan and a weary sigh, Dylan Keene snatched the De-Brainer bat from the blood splattered driveway. He stood up with a lumbering stagger, winced once from the pain that plagued his body, pulled back his aching arms and swung out, smashing the skull of the nearest Starer. The young man's head snapped to the side, his neck bent at harsh angle as he tumbled to the floor. He launched again, stopping himself too late as he caught Lucy's friend Poppy on the jaw. The young girl stumbled back, her darkening eyes cast towards the sky.

Lucy screamed and reached out for her friend who lay bleeding on the driveway.

'It isn't her Luce! Get in the car. Something's happening.'

Lucy hesitated, watching as her father indiscriminately hit another Starer with the bat. The world was wrong. Everything was wrong.

Dylan brought the De-Brainer bat down upon the crown of Martin Travis, the Keene's former milkman. The pensioner dropped to his knees. Dylan pulled on the bat, grimacing at the horrific act he'd just committed. The screw was stuck within the confines of Martin Travis's skull. With a quick debate of caution, Dylan kicked out at the kneeling man's shoulder and pulled back on the bat. The screw popped free and Dylan had his Excalibur once more.

Lucy helped her mother to her feet, shuffling towards the driver's door. Kirsty Keene started to shake off her daughter's grip. Not from protest, but from her nerves trembling. Lucy was unsure of whether it was the drugs overdose or the fear of death that caused her to quake so violently.

Behind them, more black-eyed Starers stood up and advanced with an agonisingly slow approach. Dylan cracked the heads of three more with quick succession. Bambi-legged, Poppy Smith got back on her feet, her jaw twisted out at an undesirable angle. A fresh, red flow of bloody spittle surged from her broken mouth as a cascade of crimson syrup.

Lucy pushed her impaired mother through the open driver's door and onto the passenger seat, where she slumped down, her knees buckling into the foot well. Lucy climbed between the seats into the back and called out for her father, her voice still broken from her ordeal.

'Dad! Get in!'

Dylan Keene turned. In one leaping moment he bounded into the Corsa and tossed the bat across to the passenger seat. Turning the key, and kicking the clutch the engine roared like a dying iron beast. A deep, mechanical clicking resonated from beneath the bonnet, pissing further on Dylan's bonfire. The crash against the house had dislodged something vital within the engine.

'Lock the doors. We can't let them in.'

The fuel gauge tickled red. They'd get out, but they wouldn't get far. The Starers closed in around the car as Dylan slammed it into reverse and released the clutch, revving as far as he'd dare without blowing up the engine. Bodies thumped against the bumper as the Corsa edged them out of the way. With a squeal of the tyres, Dylan backed out onto Westfield Road. More Starers bumped off the bodywork, staggering back, unfazed by the push they'd received. They stared in with oil black eyes. A chorus hands began to slap against the windows, mindless fingers waking up searching for a way in. They could just as easily smash the glass to get in. Maybe that synapse of knowledge hadn't been formed yet.

A trail had been cleared by the bus rolling down Westfield Road. Dylan gave a smile. They had a runway. They could get speed up and maybe break through. They had a chance.

Without further thought he slipped the Corsa into first and gunned the engine, they jumped forward, knocking over through a sparse crowd that gazed in over the bonnet.

Their speed increased, hitting thirty, forty, fifty. They hit a body on the road. The car didn't rock as much as he thought it would. Kristy was crying. She'd compressed down into the foot well, wrapping herself into a shaking ball of anguish and fear.

Dylan felt something stab his shoulder. With a snap of his head he glanced back. His daughter dug his nails into his shoulder, her bony knuckles deathly white. He understood why.

They reached the end of the makeshift runway. They passed the bus which had mounted the kerb coming to rest kissing the trunk of an oak tree. Dylan saw the driver's eyes. They were black.

Instinct told him to hit the horn. He didn't.

They ploughed into the crowd of people at eighty-seven miles an hour. Bodies thumped upon the Corsa, heavy as a rain of mercury and a deeper red. The windscreen cracked as more skulls and limbs thumped upon the glass. He kept his foot down and clicked the wipers on, spraying washer fluid to dilute the gore. Their vision became awash with a watery crimson, sinking them into an arterial sea. Every single body a sickening speed bump at the rate they travelled. A double thump repeated as they passed beneath both tyres with a ghastly, haunting pop.

A wiper snapped off as they hit an obese obstacle that rolled over the car roof, causing them to flinch and duck. The engine strained, bearings squealed. Dylan screamed.

Then they broke through. No light, just a sense of freedom as the sounds of death left their ears.

The remaining wiper smeared the blood enough so Dylan could see the dark road ahead. He dropped his speed a little as they turned a corner uncontested and left behind the horde that had gathered on Westfield Road. He squinted ahead, the way was clear. They'd made it out. He smiled maniacally and beat the steering wheel with his fist. He cheered at his family. They said nothing.

The black-eyed crowd shifted and turned in unison. They started to walk, slowly, as patience was their only virtue. They started to follow.

Nathan Robinson lives in Scunthorpe, England with his wife and twin boys. He writes best at night or at 77mph. In his spare time he runs through the woods, enjoys world beers and reviews for www.snakebitehorror.co.uk
He's been published in many anthologies, for the full list check him out at www.facebook.com/NathanRobinsonWrites or follow him on twitter where you'll find him as natthewriter.
Ask him anything, he'll like that.

Acknowledgements- These are the folk that shaped this story, they all mean something somehow;

I'd like to thank Mark Goddard for the Snakebite gig, Paul Johnson Jovanovic for his thoughts and opinions, everyone working and chatting on www.spinetinglers.co.uk for getting me started and liking my silly little stories (if you're a new writer, check them out), also hugs to Princess Dreamer and Kayleigh Marie Edwards for being my number one fan.

One day I'll buy a few beers for the Harlequin boys for driving whilst I wrote and for putting up with Radio 2, not forgetting Daz for stealing his dream.

A big cheer to anybody who bought a book off of the back of one of my reviews (if you've ever read a book by an indie author REVIEW IT! People read reviews before they buy a book and word of mouth is the best advertising an author can get! You thinking writing a book is hard, try getting reviews for one . . .)

Nanalaine for reading my stuff at work and not working (shhh, I won't tell anyone), the kind folks at www.pseudopod.org, Eric S Brown, Nate Burleigh and anyone who read/listened to any of my stories and enjoyed them, this is for you.

Mega thanks to folks at Severed Press for taking a chance on me and for Sutton (whoever you are) for the fierce edit and for catching all them comma's. And further thanks to Marcus Blakestone for his read through and spotting all the things that I (and everyone else) missed.

Extra special thanks to my wife Moj for finally finishing reading this with seconds to spare; you deserve a medal, my Ma 'n Pa for staying in that night and my little big men for being the funniest creatures in the universe.

Oh, and the Old Man at the Bus Stop in the Rain, all this came from you. I hope you got where you were going.

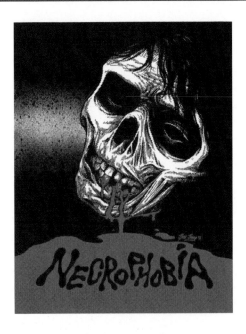

NECROPHOBIA
Jack Hamlyn

An ordinary summer's day.
The grass is green, the flowers are blooming. All is right with the world. Then the dead start rising. From cemetery and mortuary, funeral home and morgue, they flood into the streets until every town and city is infested with walking corpses, blank-eyed eating machines that exist to take down the living.

The world is a graveyard.

And when you have a family to protect, it's more than survival.

It's war!

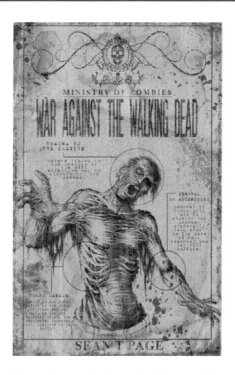

More than 63% of people now believe that there will be a global zombie apocalypse before 2050...
Employing real science and pioneering field work, War against the Walking Dead provides a complete blueprint for taking back your country from the rotting clutches of the dead after a zombie apocalypse.

* A glimpse inside the mind of the zombie using a team of top psychics - what do the walking dead think about? What lessons can we learn to help us defeat this pervading menace?
* Detailed guidelines on how to galvanise a band of scared survivors into a fighting force capable of defeating the zombies and dealing with emerging groups such as end of the world cults, raiders and even cannibals!
* Features insights from real zombie fighting organisations across the world, from America to the Philippines, Australia to China - the experts offer advice in every aspect of fighting the walking dead.
Packed with crucial zombie war information and advice, from how to build a city of the living in a land of the dead to tactics on how to use a survivor army to liberate your country from the zombies - War against the Walking Dead may be humanity's last chance.

Remember, dying is not an option!

RESURRECTION

By Tim Curran

www.corpseking.com

The rain is falling and the dead are rising. It began at an ultra-secret government laboratory. Experiments in limb regeneration-an unspeakable union of Medieval alchemy and cutting edge genetics result in the very germ of horror itself: a gene trigger that will reanimate dead tissue...any dead tissue. Now it's loose. It's gone viral. It's in the rain. And the rain has not stopped falling for weeks. As the country floods and corpses float in the streets, as cities are submerged, the evil dead are rising. And they are hungry.

"I REALLY love this book...Curran is a wonderful storyteller who really should be unleashed upon the general horror reading public sooner rather than later." – *DREAD CENTRAL*

Dead Bait

"If you don't already suffer from bathophobia and/or ichthyophobia, you probably will after reading this amazingly wonderful horrific collection of short stories about what lurks beneath the waters of the world" – *DREAD CENTRAL*

A husband hell-bent on revenge hunts a Wereshark...A Russian mail order bride with a fishy secret...Crabs with a collective consciousness...A vampire who transforms into a Candiru...Zombie piranha...Bait that will have you crawling out of your skin and more. Drawing on horror, humor with a helping of dark fantasy and a touch of deviance, these 19 contemporary stories pay homage to the monsters that lurk in the murky waters of our imaginations. *If you thought it was safe to go back in the water...Think Again!*

"Severed Press has the cojones to publish THE most outrageous, nasty and downright wonderfully disgusting horror that I've seen in quite a while." – *DREAD CENTRAL*

Zombie Zoology
Unnatural History:

Severed Press has assembled a truly original anthology
of never before published stories of living dead beasts.
Inside you will find tales of prehistoric creatures rising
from the Bog, a survivalist taking on a troop of rotting
baboons, a NASA experiment going Ape, A hunter
going a Moose too far and many more undead creatures
from Hell. The crawling, buzzing, flying abominations
of mother nature have risen and they are hungry.

"Clever and engaging a reanimated rarity"
FANGORIA

"I loved this very unique anthology and highly recommend it"
Monster Librarian

BIOHAZARD

Tim Curran

The day after tomorrow: Nuclear fallout. Mutations. Deadly pandemics. Corpse wagons. Body pits. Empty cities. The human race trembling on the edge of extinction. Only the desperate survive. One of them is Rick Nash. But there is a price for survival: communion with a ravenous evil born from the furnace of radioactive waste. It demands sacrifice. Only it can keep Nash one step ahead of the nightmare that stalks him-a sentient, seething plague-entity that stalks its chosen prey: the last of the human race. To accept it is a living death. To defy it, a hell beyond imagining

"kick back and enjoy some the most violent and genuinely scary apocalyptic horror written by one of the finest dark fiction authors plying his trade today" HORRORWORLD

www.severedpress.com

Printed in Great Britain
by Amazon.co.uk, Ltd.,
Marston Gate.